This book belongs to

Lynn Hammonds

PASSPORT
NO. 3
MYSTERIES

LOST IN
MERLIN'S
CASTLE

PASSPORT
NO. 3
MYSTERIES

LOST IN MERLIN'S CASTLE

P. J. STRAY

Silver Burdett Press
Parsippany, New Jersey

Published by Silver Burdett Press
A Division of Simon & Schuster
299 Jefferson Road
Parsippany, NJ 07054
Designed by Leslie Bauman Design

Printed in the United States of America
ISBN 0-382-39679-0 (LSB) 10 9 8 7 6 5 4 3 2 1
ISBN 0 382-39680-4 (PBK) 10 9 8 7 6 5 4 3 2 1

Library of Congress Cataloging-in-Publication Data
Stray, P. J.
Lost in Merlin's castle/by P. J. Stray
p. cm.—(A passport mystery: #3)
Summary: Stranded in the British countryside when their
van mysteriously breaks down, six teenagers find
themselves in an ancient castle, embroiled in a
centuries-old conflict between Merlin and his
enemies who seek to destroy the Earth's environment.
[1. Merlin(Legendary character)—Juvenile fiction.
[1. Merlin(Legendary character)—Fiction. 2. Magic—Fiction.
3. England—Fiction. 4. Environmental protection—Fiction.]
I. Title. II. Series: Passport mysteries: no. 3.
PZ7.S9136Lo   1996   95-15674   [Fic]—dc20 CIP   AC

CHAPTER
1

The crowd at the baggage claim milled around impatiently, waiting for their luggage to appear. A 747 carrying more than four hundred passengers from New York's Kennedy Airport had just landed at Heathrow, the main airport for London.

Four teens stood together off to the side. They had met during the flight and discovered that they were all part of the same student tour. They had talked together during most of the flight, even though it had lasted all night. The excitement of arriving kept them from being sleepy.

"What do we do now?" Elaine, a tall, blonde girl with blue eyes, asked.

Trent, a muscular, dark-haired boy in a black T-shirt and jeans, shrugged. "We wait for our bags."

He couldn't seem to stand still, cracking his knuckles and shifting from one foot to the other.

"I've been to lots of airports," a red-headed girl named Donna piped up, "but I've never seen so much confusion." She was dressed in an expensive designer outfit—a short pale blue skirt and a fitted jacket. "Back home everything is organized. There isn't even a place to sit down here."

"When we get our bags, we follow the signs to customs," Kari, a small, pretty girl with light brown skin, said, putting her brown leather backpack over her shoulder. She was wearing a long flowered sundress and denim jacket. "Then we meet this guy Axelrod on the other side of customs."

Suitcases began to appear on the conveyor belt and the crowd squeezed forward.

"I thought that there were supposed to be six of us," Donna said, flipping her long red hair off her face.

"Yeah," Trent said, turning to Kari. "What happened to those two kids you were talking to on the plane?"

"You mean Mark and Kelly?" Kari responded with a smile. "They're just stopping over here. They're going to Switzerland because they won some sort of prize. They found some old manuscript or something."

"That's what they told me, too," Elaine added, wrinkling her forehead as she tried to remember. "Something about a treasure, but it didn't make much sense. That one's mine," she said as her bag appeared.

"I'll get it," Trent announced, roughly shouldering his way through the crowd.

In a few minutes all their bags had been collected and they carried them toward customs.

"This is sure taking a long time," Donna complained. "This would never happen at the airport back home."

Kari shook her head and leaned toward Elaine. "I hope we're not going to have to listen to this the whole trip," she said in a low voice. Elaine nodded.

The customs inspectors waved them on and they walked together down a long corridor and through the exit. As they turned a corner, they saw several hundred people waiting for passengers from their flight. Many people in the waiting crowd held up handwritten signs with the name of their group or the particular people they were trying to find. The noise of the crowd was deafening.

"What do we do now?" Donna shouted over the noise, setting down her heavy bags.

"Look for Mr. Axelrod," Kari yelled back.

A tall, awkward-looking boy appeared out of the

crowd. "Are you looking for Mr. Axelrod?" he asked loudly.

All four nodded.

"I'm Dean," the tall boy said. He had blond hair and wore a plaid button-down shirt and jeans. "Mr. Axelrod is waiting over there." He pointed toward a door. "C'mon." He started to lead them, but then he noticed Donna struggling with her purse and four bags. "Let me give you a hand," he said, lifting two of her bags.

"You don't mind?" Donna asked, handing him the other two.

Dean struggled with the bags for a moment, then put one under each arm and lifted another one in each hand. "Didn't you read Mr. Axelrod's note about traveling light?" he asked as Donna walked past him carrying only her purse. "You are supposed to do what Mr. Axelrod says," he called as he struggled after her.

Mr. Axelrod was a nervous little man with a small black mustache and thick glasses with black frames. He checked their names off a list. "Just one more to find," he said, scanning the crowd. "Then we will get on our way. We have a lot of ground to cover if we are going to stay on schedule. Dean, see if you can find, uh . . ." he glanced at his list, ". . . Jeremy."

Dean walked away, and Mr. Axelrod busied himself with handing out schedules and room assignments. "We spend three days in London and then drive west into the country," he told them.

Dean returned after a few moments with a thin black student. "This is Jeremy," he announced.

Jeremy smiled shyly. He wore khaki pants, a white shirt with a blue and red striped tie, and a blue blazer. Over his shoulder he carried a large canvas bag stuffed with books and papers.

"I saw him on the plane," Elaine remarked to Kari. "He read a book practically the whole way over. He didn't speak to anyone."

"Oh, great," Trent, who had overheard Elaine and Kari, said with a sneer. "We've got some group. There's Donna the complainer, Dean the teacher's pet, and Jeremy the bookworm. What a crew!"

"This way," Mr. Axelrod said. "We've got to hurry if we're going to keep on schedule. No time to lose. We've got only three days to see London, the city of Shakespeare, Charles Dickens, and Queen Elizabeth."

"He left out Princess Di," Elaine said quietly to Kari.

CHAPTER
2

They passed through London like a whirlwind. Their first stop was the British Museum. While the others wandered though the exhibits, Jeremy got lost among the displays of books in the main library, carefully studying the rare manuscripts in their glass cases. The first printings of Shakespeare's plays fascinated him. Even though they were over four hundred years old, he had no trouble reading the words in their ornate type. He spent an especially long time looking at the Magna Carta, agreed to by King John, the king who tried to capture Robin Hood, and a copy of the first book printed in Europe with movable type, the Gutenberg Bible.

Meanwhile, Mr. Axelrod led the others on a quick tour. The marble statues created for the

Parthenon in ancient Greece took their breath away. Called the "Elgin Marbles" after Lord Elgin, a British diplomat who "rescued" the statues and brought them to England, they show a parade of people, mythological creatures, and horses that look so real they seem to move. "The Greek government wants them back," Mr. Axelrod said. "Every year they ask the British government for their return. But the British claim they are keeping them 'safe.'"

They followed Mr. Axelrod through a room lined with stone walls from ancient Assyria. The carvings showed men with bows and arrows hunting lions from chariots. "These are from ancient Nimrud, in Turkey," Mr. Axelrod announced. "They're almost 3,000 years old."

They passed two statues shaped like huge winged bulls but with human heads. "They look like something out of a nightmare," Dean remarked with a shudder.

"But this stuff is so old!" Donna said with a pout. "When do we get to do something fun?"

Elaine nudged Kari with her elbow and smiled slyly. "The fun stuff comes later, trust me."

They found Jeremy bending over the display showing the Rosetta Stone, trying to make out the writing carved on it.

"Where'd you come from?" Dean asked.

"This is on my list of things I must see," Jeremy replied. "It's one of the most important documents in history."

"Looks like a black stone to me," Trent interjected. "When do we go to the Tower of London?"

"When do we eat?" Donna asked.

Mr. Axelrod waved them together. "Hurry now," he said rapidly. "This stone was discovered by scientists traveling with Napoleon when he invaded Egypt. It was captured by the British after they defeated Napoleon at the Battle of the Nile. The stone is carved with the same words in three different languages—Egyptian hieroglyphic writing, ancient Greek, and another form of Egyptian. Since scholars could already understand Greek, they were able to unravel the meaning of Egyptian hieroglyphic writing. The Rosetta Stone is the key to almost everything we know about ancient Egypt."

"When do we get to go shopping?" Donna asked.

Mr. Axelrod glanced at his watch. "Not now. We're going to eat, but we have to hurry if we are going to get to the Tower of London before it closes. Please stay together."

Mr. Axelrod led the way across the street. "Make sure you look to the right first," he said. "Remember that the British drive on the right side of the road."

"You mean the wrong side," Donna chirped. "We drive on the right side back home."

They walked past rows of four- and five-story residences, faced in dark brick, then crossed a square with large shady trees. "This is Russell Square," Mr. Axelrod said, "in the heart of Bloomsbury. This is where many famous writers and philosophers lived at the beginning of the Twentieth Century. The novelist Virginia Woolf and her husband lived here."

"When do we eat?" Elaine asked.

"All right, all right," Mr. Axelrod replied. "There's a pub just around the corner."

"A pub?" Dean asked. "Do you think we should eat in a bar, Mr. Axelrod?"

"Oh, it's not really a bar," Mr. Axelrod said, "or at least not in the American sense. They sell beer, but they also sell food."

"I just want to know," Trent said, "if I can get a hamburger and fries."

"Now we've been through this before," Mr. Axelrod responded, stopping on the sidewalk. "I promised your parents that you would get the real feel of England. Eating fast food is not going to give you that experience."

"You can probably get chips," Dean added. "That's what they call French fries."

Mr. Axelrod led them into a pub and they found

an empty table near a window. The room was paneled in dark wood and it had a carpeted floor. A dartboard hung in one corner.

There was no table service so they had to go up to the bar and order their food. Jeremy and Dean had the same meal as Mr. Axelrod: sliced roast beef, mashed potatoes, and green peas. Elaine and Trent had fish and chips, and Kari and Donna tried a Welsh pasty, a kind of baked turnover filled with meat. They all drank tea.

"I'd rather have pizza," Donna remarked after she took a bite of the Welsh pasty.

"I can't get used to this money," Elaine said as she put away her change from lunch.

"Yeah," Dean agreed, " the bills are all different colors."

"And sizes," Kari added.

"The higher the value, the bigger the banknote," Mr. Axelrod said.

"Boy," Jeremy chimed in, "imagine what a million-pound note must look like." He held his hands wide apart. "It would be like a sheet of wallpaper."

The others laughed.

Mr. Axelrod looked at his watch. "My goodness," he said. "I had no idea it was so late."

"But it's only three o'clock," Dean commented. "How come the pub is closing?"

"Pubs are closed from three to five in the after-noon," Mr. Axelrod replied. "We have to hurry anyway if we're going to have time to see the Tower of London."

"Cool!" Trent exclaimed. "Finally, we get to see the Tower."

"But I want to see Harrod's," Donna complained. "I don't want to see any old tower."

"How about seeing the Crown Jewels?" Jeremy asked, looking at his list.

"Fabulous," Donna responded enthusiastically. "I'd love to see them."

"Well," Jeremy continued, "the Crown Jewels are in the Tower of London."

As they walked out of the restaurant, Elaine asked Kari, "What's Harrods?"

"It's a big department store." Kari replied.

"Duh," Donna added, looking cross-eyed at Elaine. "Everybody knows about Harrods."

"Oh," Elaine replied, rolling her eyes. "Right."

They traveled by taxi to the Tower, passing through Piccadilly Circus. The name made Elaine laugh. "It's not a circus at all," she said in amusement. "It's just a traffic circle."

The Tower of London loomed above the group, black and foreboding. A guard dressed in a bright red uniform pointed to a line of people, shouting, "This way, please. This way."

"We have to stand in line?" Donna asked in a complaining tone.

"It's a queue," Dean said.

"What?" Donna asked.

"The British call it a queue, not a line."

"Oh."

They stood in the queue for a long time, but finally another guide dressed in a red uniform led them on a tour around the Tower's massive walls and moats, and told them it's bloody history.

"The Tower is really a group of buildings built over hundreds of years," the guide told them. "It was started by William the Conqueror after he defeated the Saxons in 1066. It has been added to by many kings, including Richard the Lionhearted. Many great English men and women have spent time in the Tower, often as prisoners. Anne Boleyn, Sir Walter Raleigh, and Sir Thomas More were beheaded here. And the Nazi leader Rudolf Hess was confined here during World War II."

They followed the guide across the grassy courtyard toward the building that housed the Crown Jewels. He paused near a raised wooden platform with a large block of wood on it. "This is the location where Lady Jane Grey was beheaded. It's a very sad story. She became Queen of England after the death of Henry VIII but her reign lasted only nine days. She was overthrown by Mary I—Bloody Mary as she is now known. Lady Jane was beheaded at the age of sixteen. Her young husband was also beheaded shortly after. We will see the room where he was imprisoned and the place where he carved Lady Jane's name on the wall of his cell."

"That sounds romantic," Kari whispered to Elaine.

Several very fat, glossy black ravens walked toward them. "Get those birds away from me," Donna exclaimed. "They're so dirty."

The guide cleared his throat loudly. "These ravens live in the Tower," he said. "There are six of them and they are fed every day. Legend says that when the ravens depart, the Tower will fall. So far, the ravens have stayed and so has the Tower."

The others stared at Donna. "Well, I didn't know," she said huffily, and followed the guide across the courtyard to the line of people waiting to see the Crown Jewels.

"You know," Jeremy said, "ravens can talk."

"I wonder what they'd say about Donna," Elaine commented.

The line waiting to see the Crown Jewels was long, but it seemed to move quickly enough. They were led through two doorways with huge polished metal doors. The first room contained massive silver plates, cups, and great silver maces and swords. Trent tried to stop to look closely at the swords, but the guards told him to keep moving.

The Crown Jewels were in the next room, more brilliant in the bright lights than they had expected. The guards herded them through quickly, but Jeremy managed to point out several things that were on his list. "The Royal Scepter has the largest diamond ever cut, one of the Stars of Africa found in 1905." He also pointed out the large ruby on the Imperial State Crown that dated back to the Black Prince in the 1360's.

"That ruby was probably worn by King Henry V at the Battle of Agincourt," Mr. Axelrod added. "That's where a small army of English archers defeated a huge French army of mounted knights. Shakespeare's play *Henry V* tells all about it."

"Please hurry along," a guard announced. "You are holding up the queue."

"Whew!" Kari remarked as they stepped back outside into the courtyard, "that was fast."

"I barely got to see anything," Donna whined.

"Okay, everyone," said Trent, "it's on to the dungeon."

CHAPTER
3

The group entered the dungeon. It was dark and filled with strange shapes hidden in the shadows.

"Should it really be this dark in here?" Donna asked nervously.

"I don't think it should," Mr. Axelrod said. "Something must have happened to the lights. I'd better go tell one of the guards."

Dean paused uncertainly for a moment and then scuttled after Mr. Axelrod.

"All right!" Trent said, striding into the room. "Let's take a look at this stuff."

He stood next to a table made out of thick beams of wood with a set of pulleys at each end. "This must be the rack," he said. "They stretched people with these ropes to get them to confess."

Kari and Elaine had wandered over to a mummy-shaped contraption with sharp nails pointing out from the inside. "What's this?" Kari asked.

Donna came over and leaned close to the label on the exhibit. "It's called an Iron Maiden," she read, squinting her eyes in the darkness. "It looks pretty scary to me."

"I guess you'd stick around if you got in there," Trent remarked with a laugh.

Jeremy didn't seem very interested. "These don't look real," he said. "They all look like fakes."

"They look real enough to me," Donna responded with a shudder.

"What's this lead to?" Elaine asked, pointing to a small door off to the side.

Jeremy and Trent walked over to her.

"I'll bet it's the entrance to the forget-me-not," Jeremy said.

"What's a forget-me-not?" Trent asked.

"It's a small cell in the back of a dungeon. Unwanted prisoners were put there and forgotten."

"How do you know all this stuff?" Trent asked.

"I read about it on the plane."

"Hey, look," Elaine said, pulling on the door. "It opens."

The weak light from the dungeon barely penetrated the dark doorway.

"Wonder what's inside?" Trent asked.

"Why don't you take a little peek through the door?" Elaine suggested.

Trent peered into the doorway.

"I'll bet we aren't supposed to go in there," Jeremy said.

"Yeah," Trent agreed. "It's probably off-limits to visitors."

"You afraid?" Elaine asked.

"No," Trent replied uncertainly.

"Are you chicken?" Elaine taunted, flapping her arms like wings. "Cluck, cluck, cluck . . ."

"No," Trent said decisively. He grabbed Jeremy by the arm. "C'mon, let's see what's inside."

They stepped into the small cell, and the door slammed behind them.

"Gotcha!" Elaine shouted gleefully.

The lights in the dungeon came on suddenly and a guard and Mr. Axelrod appeared, followed by Dean.

"There," Mr. Axelrod said. "That's much better."

Trent and Jeremy pounded on the door of their cell. "Hey! Let us out!" they shouted.

"Where are the boys?" Mr. Axelrod asked Elaine and Kari.

"I think they went somewhere they shouldn't have," Elaine replied.

The guard walked straight up to the door of the forget-me-not and pulled it open. "You boys should not be in there!" he said gruffly. He turned to Mr. Axelrod. "Are these boys with you? I'm afraid I will have to ask you to leave the Tower. This kind of misbehavior cannot be tolerated. We just cannot have it!"

Mr. Axelrod looked embarrassed. "Of course," he said. "I'll take them out right away. And I assure you, they will be punished."

"But . . ." Trent started to say.

"You keep quiet," Mr. Axelrod said heatedly. "You've done quite enough for one day."

"I'll make sure that you find your way out," the guard said huffily. "Please follow me and stay close."

Kari whispered to Elaine as they walked across the courtyard toward the exit, "That was a mean trick."

"Yeah," Elaine replied, "but it was funny."

CHAPTER
4

The wind came in great gusts, driving the pouring rain hard against the minivan. Mr. Axelrod was hunched over the steering wheel, trying to see through the storm. Rows of tall trees arched over the road, turning it into a black tunnel. The headlights revealed nothing but the narrow country road awash with rain.

Dean checked the map again and peered out the front window. They were supposed to be driving west, nearing the border between England and Wales, but they hadn't seen a road sign or even a light in nearly two hours. Dean had no idea where they were, but Mr. Axelrod kept driving doggedly onward.

Jeremy was the only person in the back of the

van who seemed to be awake. He sat in the second row of seats with Elaine. Donna was snoring softly next to Kari in the third row. Trent was next to them, folded tightly into a corner with his head leaning at an odd angle. All of them were exhausted from their whirlwind three-day tour of London.

Donna and Kari had complained loudly about how tired their feet were from all the walking. But the boys were especially tired. Someone had played another practical joke on them by arranging for the hotel to give them a wake-up call at five o'clock in the morning, telling them to hurry. They had dressed, packed their bags, and arrived downstairs to meet Mr. Axelrod in the lobby by quarter of six. By the time Mr. Axelrod and the girls finally appeared at about eight o'clock, they had been waiting for over two hours. Elaine whispered "Gotcha!" when she saw them.

The boys realized they had been tricked, but they were almost too embarrassed to tell Mr. Axelrod what had happened. When they finally did, Mr. Axelrod took the girls aside and told them that there would be no more practical jokes. But the girls all looked so innocent, Mr. Axelrod wasn't sure what had happened. He wondered if perhaps the hotel had made a mistake.

"Are we lost?" Jeremy asked in a low voice.

Mr. Axelrod reached over the steering wheel and cleaned the fog off the windshield with his hand. "No," he said. "We'll get our bearings as soon as this rain stops."

Another gust of wind shook the minivan, but the rain seemed to be tapering off.

"Dean," Mr. Axelrod said, "look on the map near Glastonbury. That was the last sign I saw. We should be somewhere near there by now."

Jeremy sat up and leaned forward. Elaine, still asleep in the next seat, stirred and then settled back.

Dean turned the map around, looking for Glastonbury.

"It's down here," Jeremy said, leaning over the back of the front seat and pointing at the map.

Dean moved the map so he could see the place where Jeremy pointed. "If that's where we are, then we're too far south. Wales is up here."

"But Glastonbury is one of the places I want to see," Jeremy said. "It's supposed to be where King Arthur is buried."

"The Round-Table guy?" Dean asked.

"Yeah. Some monks found his tomb there hundreds of years ago."

"But that's all a myth," Mr. Axelrod interjected. "There never was any King Arthur or Merlin or . . . a Round Table."

Suddenly there was a deafening explosion and a blinding white light filled the minivan.

The brakes of the van screeched as it spun out of control on the wet pavement, finally skidding to a stop under a huge tree at the side of the road.

The glare of the white inside the van dazzled Jeremy and Dean.

"What is it?" Dean shouted in terror.

The light vanished, leaving them in darkness.

CHAPTER
5

"What was that!" Trent exclaimed from the back of the van.

"Did we hit something?" Donna asked, sitting up quickly.

"How come it's so dark?" Jeremy asked.

The minivan's headlights had gone out and the engine was silent. Mr. Axelrod turned the key and tried to start the engine.

Nothing happened.

He tried again, shifting the gear lever and pushing buttons on the dashboard. The minivan remained silent. Even the rain had stopped.

"All right," Mr. Axelrod said, unfastening his seat belt. "We'd better take a look under the hood."

"You mean the bonnet," Dean said. "That's what the British call it."

"That's enough." Mr. Axelrod was not amused. "Let's just check the engine. Jeremy, bring your flashlight."

Everyone climbed out of the minivan. Elaine and Donna stood by the side of the road while Kari and the boys looked at the engine with Mr. Axelrod.

Jeremy grabbed his canvas bag and went to the front of the minivan. He pulled out his flashlight and pointed at the engine.

Mr. Axelrod reached into the engine and tugged experimentally on some wires. "Nothing seems to be loose," he said.

"Check the carburetor and the air filter," Trent said. "That's what I always do."

"There isn't any carburetor to fix," Kari said knowingly. "This engine has fuel injection."

Trent pulled back in surprise. "How do you know that?"

"My dad taught me. You thought I wouldn't know anything just because I'm a girl, didn't you?"

"N-no," Trent said defensively. "That's not what I meant . . . ."

"I think it has something to do with the electrical system," Mr. Axelrod said. "Even the headlights are out."

"Mr. Axelrod," Elaine called, "look over there. There's a light."

They all turned toward where Elaine pointed. Through the trees along the road they could just make out a single bright light.

"It's not a star?" Dean asked.

"Not in this weather," Trent said gruffly.

"Maybe it's a nice comfortable motel," Donna said hopefully. "With clean sheets and a hot bath."

"C'mon," Mr. Axelrod said. "There's got to be someone there who can help us. Just remember that we left the van under this big tree."

The light was closer than it seemed, but as they walked toward it along the wet road, it seemed to rise into the air. Slowly the shadowy shape of a huge dark castle appeared in front of them. Its walls and turrets seemed to loom over them threateningly as they made their way across the muddy ground. The light was coming from a window high in one of the castle's towers.

The light flickered for a moment as a dark figure passed in front of it.

"Someone's there," Kari said. "There he is again."

"I see him," Dean responded as the light flickered again.

"Look out!" Jeremy warned. Everyone stopped.

Jeremy pointed his flashlight ahead of them. They were approaching the edge of a deep moat. "Watch where you walk," Jeremy continued. "You could fall in there pretty easily." His flashlight reflected weakly off the water below.

"Let's find the entrance," Mr. Axelrod said.

They followed the walls around until they came to a drawbridge that stretched across the moat. "This is way cool," Jeremy said.

"I think it's creepy," Donna commented.

"C'mon," Mr. Axelrod said, "we've got to find some help."

As they walked across the drawbridge to a heavy wooden door framed in a large stone arch, rain started to fall again. Mr. Axelrod searched for a knocker, but there wasn't one.

"Maybe there's a doorbell," Donna suggested.

"Aw, c'mon," Kari said with disgust. "This is a castle. You have to knock loudly to wake the servants."

"Where'd you get that?" Dean asked.

"From a movie," Kari replied with a smile as she took off one of her hiking boots. She began pounding loudly on the door with the boot.

"Hold it," Mr. Axelrod said after a moment. "That's enough noise to wake up the dead."

"I hear someone coming . . ." Dean said. "At least I think I do."

There was a rattling sound and then a scraping of metal. They all pulled back from the door.

A small door set into the large wooden door opened and a man holding a candelabra with several burning candles leaned through. "What do you want?" he demanded.

Mr. Axelrod hesitated and then stepped forward. "Our van broke down. We're stuck on the road down below here. We'd like to use your phone."

"We haven't got a phone." The man glared at them with his dark eyes. He was large and muscular and completely bald. He wore a formal jacket with long tails and striped pants. He pulled back and began to close the door.

"Uh," Mr. Axelrod said uncertainly, "then maybe you can tell us where we can find one."

"Maybe you can let us come in and get dry," Donna said quickly. "My hair is a mess."

"Who is it, Percival?" another man's voice called from inside.

The man at the door turned back. "Just some travelers looking for a phone, sir."

"Well, let them come in out of the rain," the voice from inside said.

The man paused for a moment in the doorway and seemed to notice the rain for the first time. "Yes," he said, stepping back, "of course. It's been so long since we've had visitors, I've quite forgotten my manners." He stepped back into the castle and held the candelabra high. "Please. Come in out of the elements."

Mr. Axelrod led them through the doorway. As they entered, a strange cold gripped them, making them shiver.

"Whew," Donna remarked, "it's colder in here than outside."

Elaine stayed back with Kari, who was putting her boot back on. Kari stood up and started to enter. Then she noticed Elaine. Elaine's face was white and her eyes darted from side to side.

"Is something wrong?" Kari asked. "You look really scared."

Elaine shook her head slowly. "No. . . I guess I'm all right. There's just something weird . . . I've got a strange feeling."

"C'mon, Elaine!" Trent said impatiently, leaning back through the door. "Stop trying to scare us. We've had enough of your stupid tricks."

CHAPTER
6

An old man with a white beard stood just inside the doorway peering at them through thick glasses. He wore a maroon jacket and plaid vest over a starched white shirt. He had a sad and careworn look about him, bent and fragile. His voice was shaky and frail.

The old man pulled nervously at his white beard. "My name is . . . uh . . . Professor Emrys," he said. "And this is my man, Percival. You'll have to excuse his lack of hospitality. He's always on guard for intruders. Please do come in and warm yourselves by the fire."

The professor and Percival led them down a long hallway lined with dull gray suits of armor holding lances and swords. Other weapons, including bows, spears, battle-axes, and more swords, adorned the walls. Great banners and battle flags hung from poles near the ceiling.

They walked through another door and into a huge dining hall. Its rafters were draped with flags, and one wall was covered by a colorful tapestry showing men in armor hunting a unicorn. Across from the tapestry was a large fireplace with a crackling fire burning logs that looked too large to lift. But what was in the center of the room grabbed their attention: an enormous round table that could seat fifty or more. At its center were five gold candelabras, each holding dozens of candles. Around the candelabras stood silver bowls and serving dishes. And around the edge of the table were plates and goblets, with forks and knives, all made of sparkling gold, encrusted with jewels.

Trent whistled softly.

The others stayed back, admiring the room, but Donna walked right up to a jeweled throne, which was much more ornate than the other seats at the table. She picked up a goblet and said, "This is better than the Crown Jewels. You can touch this stuff."

"Young lady," Percival said anxiously, "please."

"Donna!" Mr. Axelrod said sharply.

Professor Emrys seemed amused for a moment. "You must be cold and hungry," he said. "This is the Great Hall of this castle. It is a little large for getting acquainted. Come into the library and Percival will fetch you something to eat. And perhaps some tea?"

He led the way through a side door and into a room lined from floor to ceiling with books. Piles of books were stacked in the corners and scattered on the floor. Several comfortable chairs and wooden tables were also covered with old books and papers.

"Wow!" Jeremy said. "What is this place?"

Professor Emrys gestured toward a large desk. "This is where I carry on my investigations."

"Investigations of what?" Mr. Axelrod asked.

"Oh," the professor replied, "investigations of many things. Many, many things."

Trent picked up a jar from one of the tables. "Look at this," he said, thrusting the jar at Elaine and Donna.

They shied back. "It's a bug!" Donna squealed.

"Please don't," Mr. Axelrod said.

"No, no, it's quite all right," the professor interjected. "That's one of the mysteries that concerns me now." He took the bottle from Trent and held it up so they could all see it. "Look carefully."

"All I see is a black moth," Dean said in his matter-of-fact tone. "There's no mystery about that."

The professor put down the jar and flipped over the heavy pages of an old book that lay open on one of the tables. He opened it to a drawing of another moth, only this one was white. "Look here," he said. "This is the same kind of moth, only this drawing was made over a hundred years ago. How could a moth change its color?"

"Who cares," Trent whispered to Kari.

Kari punched him in the shoulder. "Don't be a jerk."

Percival entered with tea and sandwiches and they all swarmed around the silver platter. For a few moments no one spoke as the professor watched them eat.

Suddenly the door to the library opened and a tall woman dressed in a long white satin gown appeared. A white veil concealed her face, but not her striking blonde hair. She moved with a smooth grace across the room without looking to the left or right. She paused and then opened another door and exited. The door closed behind her.

"Who was that?" Donna burst out.

"She didn't even seem to know we were here," Dean remarked.

Percival cleared his throat. "That is Lady Viviane, the owner of this castle. I'm afraid the . . . the Lady . . . ah . . . isn't quite herself tonight."

Elaine walked slowly over to the door where Lady Viviane had gone through. "I feel like I've seen her somewhere before," she murmured to no one in particular. Elaine seemed almost dazed.

Mr. Axelrod looked closely at Elaine. "You look like you could use some sleep."

Percival clapped his hands loudly. "I've prepared some rooms for you to spend the night. Time for me to show you to your rooms. I'm sure you will find them comfortable. This way, please." He directed them toward the door through which they entered. Jeremy was the last to leave. As he passed through the door he said to himself, "Where are my manners," and turned to say good night to the professor.

The library was empty. The professor was gone!

CHAPTER
7

Jeremy hurried to catch up with the others. Percival led them through the Great Hall to a wide, curving staircase. About halfway up the stairs stood Professor Emrys. He was wearing a robe of some sort. It looked black but became a dark purple when it caught the light.

"How did he do that?" Jeremy exclaimed.

"Do what?" Kari asked, but before he could answer the professor began to speak.

"Would you like to see some magic?" the professor asked. His voice seemed much stronger. He even looked younger. "My visitors have always been rather keen on magic."

"I've always loved magic," Elaine said dreamily.

Kari looked at her strangely. "Are you all right?" she asked.

Elaine slowly nodded. "I'm fine," she said. "I just love tricks, that's all."

"Yeah," Dean commented. "We know about you and your tricks."

"This one was very popular . . . uh . . . some time ago," the professor said as he raised his arms into the air above his head. He gestured strangely. "And ye shall have music!" he chanted twice slowly, pronouncing each syllable. Then he said words none of them could understand.

There was a moment of silence and then the sound of flutes and drums came out of the air. The music was soft and slow at first, but slowly the volume and the tempo increased.

"Bor-ing!" Trent said loudly.

"My disc player sounds better than that," Donna said.

"I kind of like it," Mr. Axelrod remarked. "It makes me feel relaxed."

"Where's the stereo hidden?" Kari asked. "I've got some discs that could make this castle rock!"

The professor looked crestfallen. He dropped his hands to his sides. The music stopped.

Percival took several steps up the stairs.

"Wait a moment," the professor said. "What

about this?" He clapped his hands and the lights went out, plunging them into darkness. Donna shrieked in surprise. Jeremy pulled his flashlight out of his canvas bag and shined it at the professor.

The professor smiled and clapped his hands again. The lights came back on.

"Well?" he asked.

Trent smirked. "It's just a sound-activated gadget you hook up to the light switch."

"We've all seen it advertised on TV dozens of times," Kari added.

"Yeah," Donna chimed in. "My grandmother even has one."

The professor seemed to deflate before their eyes. Instead of the tall, strong person they had been watching, he became the frail, bent figure they had met earlier. "This is very disappointing," he murmured. He turned and walked slowly up the stairs and out of sight.

"Come along, now," Percival said, and he led them to the second floor.

The hall was lined with heavy furniture and more suits of armor, but everything seemed dusty, as though no one had been there in a long time.

"Boy," Jeremy said, "you could outfit an army with all this stuff."

Percival glanced at Jeremy sharply but said

nothing. He opened one of the many doors that lined the hallway and announced, "The young gentlemen will stay in this room." Pointing across the hall, he said to Mr. Axelrod, "You, sir, will sleep in this room, and the young ladies will each have separate rooms down the hall."

The room the boys entered was very large and dimly lit. A fireplace filled one corner, but it was empty and the room was cold. There were three beds with canopies and heavy velvet spreads that hung down to the stone floor. When Trent slapped one of the beds, a cloud of dust rose up.

"Gross," he said, "I hope nobody has allergies."

"We probably will after tonight," Dean commented ruefully.

"This place is really weird," Jeremy said.

"This place?" Trent replied, "Don't you mean these people? They're the weird ones."

"What do you think that old professor was up to with all that magic stuff?" Dean asked.

"And that woman who wandered through," Trent added. "She was spooky."

"That name," Jeremy mused, "I know I've heard it or read it somewhere . . ."

"You mean the professor's?" Dean asked.

"Yeah," Jeremy replied. "Professor Emrys. I just can't remember . . ."

"What are we going to sleep in?" Dean asked. "All our clothes are in the van."

"You'll just have to rough it," Trent replied, "and sleep in your clothes."

They climbed into their beds. After a moment Trent sat up and said, "One of you guys has to get up and shut the lights off."

No one moved.

"One of you guys better shut off the lights," Trent said in a threatening tone.

"Okay, okay," Dean finally said. "Where's the switch?"

"What switch?" Jeremy asked. "In this place you just clap your hands." He clapped loudly.

The lights went off.

"Wow!" Dean exclaimed.

"Do that again," Trent said.

Jeremy clapped and the lights came back on.

"Cool!" Trent exclaimed.

"Let me try it," Dean said. He clapped and the lights went off again. Then they were all clapping and laughing loudly as the lights flashed on and off.

After a few moments they stopped clapping and settled down.

Suddenly, the lights began to flash rapidly—on their own.

CHAPTER
8

The boys yelled as the lights flashed.

There was a knock at the door and the room went dark.

The door opened and Mr. Axelrod stuck his head in. "Have any of you seen the keys to the van?"

"No," they all replied.

"Maybe you should ask Elaine?" Trent said to Mr. Axelrod sarcastically.

"Maybe you left the keys in the van," Dean suggested.

"Yes," Mr. Axelrod said sheepishly, "that's what I was afraid of."

Trent clapped his hands and the lights came on.

"So that's how they work," Mr. Axelrod said. "I couldn't find a switch in my room."

"They must have these gadgets in all the rooms in this place," Trent commented.

"I wonder where the light is coming from," Dean said.

"Maybe it's indirect lighting," Jeremy suggested.

"Indirect is right," Dean said. "It doesn't seem to come from anywhere."

"I'm going out to check the van," Mr. Axelrod said. "I want to find those keys and make sure it's all locked up."

"Can we come along?" Dean asked. "I'd like to get something to sleep in."

"Sure," Mr. Axelrod replied. "Anyway, I need Jeremy's light."

"I'll get it," Jeremy said. He reached for his jacket, which he had left on a chair. Something small scurried away. "What's that?" he asked, quickly pulling his hand back.

A brown mouse scampered across the floor to the corner with the fireplace. It paused there and turned to stare at them.

"Where'd he come from?" Trent asked.

"I'm sure every castle has mice," Mr. Axelrod said. "They're probably scared of us and stay out of sight."

The mouse cocked its head and seemed to listen

to their conversation. They could see white fur on its face, almost like a human beard.

"This one doesn't seem very scared," Trent said. He jumped off his bed toward the mouse.

The mouse didn't move.

Trent suddenly shouted at the mouse. The mouse still didn't run away. "See," Trent said. "It's not afraid."

"Enough, Trent!" Mr. Axelrod said. "Leave the poor thing alone."

Mr. Axelrod led the way out into the hall toward the stairs.

"Look," Trent said, pointing toward the doorway. "It's following us."

The mouse was sitting in the doorway, watching them.

Trent stealthily picked up a pillow from a chair in the hall. With a shout, he suddenly hurled it toward the mouse.

The mouse dodged out of the way of the pillow, but it didn't run away.

"Come on, Trent," Dean said. "A mouse can't hurt you."

"I know that," Trent said, turning on Dean. "I just don't like anyone spying on me."

"A mouse can't spy," Dean said.

"Well, it sure looks like it's spying," Trent

replied, and followed Mr. Axelrod down the stairs to the main hall.

Dean shrugged at Jeremy and went downstairs. Jeremy stood lost in thought for a moment and then followed the others down to the front hall and the door. He glanced back and saw that the small brown mouse was still watching.

CHAPTER
9

Outside the rain had stopped and the air smelled fresh and clean after the mustiness of the castle.

Mr. Axelrod took a deep breath. "Whew! That's better," he said as he looked around. The full moon was shining so brightly it seemed almost like daylight. "I guess I didn't need your light after all, Jeremy."

Dean pointed at the ground. "Look," he said, "you can see the footprints we left when we walked to the castle."

The trail of their footprints was clearly visible in the mud, disappearing around the curve of the road.

"C'mon," Mr. Axelrod said. "We won't have any trouble finding the van in this light."

A cloud floated across the moon, its shadow darkening the road. Jeremy turned on his flashlight.

They followed their tracks along the road in silence, looking for the minivan.

"This seems longer than I remember," Dean said.

"We haven't come to that big tree where we left the van yet," Jeremy said. "This is the only road." He shined the light downward. "And there are our tracks."

"No way we could be lost," Trent added.

They followed the road around several curves. The sky cleared and the moonlight became brighter. There before them was the tree they were looking for.

"Where's the van?" Dean asked, scratching his head.

The minivan was gone!

"Are you sure that this is the right tree?" Trent asked.

"It sure looks like it," Dean said.

"It is," Jeremy said decisively. "Look at the ground." He pointed his light near the trunk of the tree. "Our tracks start right here."

There was a muddle of footprints that eventually led back toward the castle.

Mr. Axelrod was dismayed. "I must have left the

keys and somebody stole it."

Jeremy looked around. Except for the small light from the castle, there was no sign of life. "Who would have stolen it?" he wondered out loud.

Dean squatted down. "We can figure this out," he said. "All we have to do is find the clues." He peered intently at the footprints. "Jeremy, let me borrow your flashlight."

"Stop pretending you're a detective," Trent said. "You aren't going to find anything."

"Oh, yeah?" Dean replied. "Look here." He pointed the flashlight at the tracks left by the van's wheels. "These tire tracks go that way . . . toward the castle."

"Maybe someone took it there for safekeeping," Mr. Axelrod suggested.

Dean followed the tire tracks toward the castle. After a few yards he stopped and whistled. "What do you think happened here?"

The tire tracks ended. Dean, Jeremy, and Mr. Axelrod stood looking at the end of the tracks in amazement.

"What is this?" Mr. Axelrod said, scratching his head. "No van. And now no tracks?"

"Aw, come on!" Trent said, pushing past them. "It's simple. Whoever took the van just drove it back onto the pavement. It wouldn't leave any tracks on hard cement. I'll show you." He stepped forward to where the tracks ended and took several steps. His feet sunk deep into the mud, filling his shoes with water. "Aarghh!" he shouted as he pitched forward into the mud.

Mr. Axelrod helped Trent out of the mud. Trent's pants and sleeves were wet with mud where he had caught his fall with his hands and knees. A threatening look from Trent was all that kept Dean and Jeremy from exploding with laughter.

Jeremy pointed his light at the tracks again. "It looks like the van just sort of took off and flew."

CHAPTER
10

As they stood looking at where the tracks ended, the moonlight slowly faded. Jeremy was the first to notice. "What's going on?" he asked as he swung his flashlight around in the darkness.

A cloud of mist had gathered between them and the castle. The light in the tower seemed to waver as the mist swept by.

"We'd better get back," Mr. Axelrod said, "before we lose sight of that light and get lost."

As they walked toward the castle, the mist seemed to make it move in the moonlight. The castle seemed to slowly fade away, its walls and battlements disappearing into the darkness. Then the mist cleared slightly and the walls reappeared, shimmering in the moonlight.

"It's like a tug of war," Dean remarked. "Like someone is trying to hide the castle and something keeps pulling it back into sight."

Trent shook his head in disgust. "You're really going off the deep end," he said.

"It's weird," Jeremy added. "When it glows like that, it looks like it's radioactive."

"Maybe it's magic," Trent taunted.

"Don't be silly," Mr. Axelrod responded. "It's just the moonlight. We'd better hurry along and get inside." He moved briskly ahead.

"We've walked a lot farther than when we came," Dean said after several minutes, "and the castle isn't getting any closer."

"What?" Trent exclaimed. "Now you're going to tell me the castle is running away from us?" He slapped his muddy pants for emphasis. "You're seeing things!"

"Nothing to worry about," Mr. Axelrod responded mildly. "The way back always seems longer. It's getting colder. Let's hurry up." He broke into a jog.

Finally they reached the castle. Mr. Axelrod led them across the drawbridge and up the stairs to the castle's huge main door. He banged on the door.

After a few moments, Percival answered. He spoke sternly. "You shouldn't be wandering about.

Things have been known to happen to visitors at night. Please stay in your rooms."

Trent clapped his hands as they entered their room. The lights came on.

"Home sweet home," Dean said.

"Home dusty home," Trent responded, throwing his jacket on a chair.

Jeremy heard a rustling sound. He glanced at his canvas bag on the floor near his bed and caught sight of the brown mouse scampering toward a hole at the base of the wall. The mouse paused at the entrance to the hole and looked back at him. The white of its face made its small black eyes seem to peer directly into his. A thought suddenly occurred to Jeremy: this was no ordinary mouse. There was intelligence in those bright eyes.

"Will you be needing anything further, sir?" Percival asked very loudly, interrupting Jeremy's thoughts.

Jeremy was suddenly very thirsty. "Could I have a glass of water?" he asked.

Trent sneered at him, "Does little baby need a drinkie?"

Percival ignored Trent. "I'll get it for you, sir."

The three boys pulled back the heavy covers on their beds, resigned to sleeping in their clothes. A short while later Percival brought a glass of water on

49

a small silver tray. Jeremy thanked him.

"Will that be all?" Percival asked. Then he left, closing the door behind him.

Trent clapped his hands and the lights went out. "These gadgets are amazing," he commented in the darkness.

"I still wonder where the light is coming from," Dean replied. "I haven't seen a single lamp in any room we've been in."

"Maybe it's . . ." Jeremy began.

"Maybe it's magic," Trent interrupted. "Now go to sleep already."

CHAPTER
11

Jeremy woke suddenly. The room was dark, lit only by the pale moonlight coming through the window. He rolled over in his bed.

"You awake?" Dean asked.

"Yeah. What is it?"

"I don't know," Dean replied, "but something's wrong."

"Will you guys shut up!" Trent said irritably. "I finally get to sleep in this dusty, lumpy contraption and. . ."

"What time is it?" Jeremy asked.

Trent reached for his watch on the table next to his bed. The watch was gone. "Which one of you turkeys stole my watch?" he demanded angrily.

"My radio is missing, too," Dean said, searching next to his bed. "Turn on the lights!"

Trent clapped his hands.

No lights came on.

He clapped again. No lights.

Jeremy and Dean tried clapping, but the lights wouldn't come on.

They all tried together. Nothing. They glanced apprehensively at each other in the dim light.

"Something's wrong," Dean said. "I can feel it."

Jeremy went to his bag and pulled out his flashlight. He swept the room with the light.

"Nothing wrong that I can see," Trent said.

Some movement caught Jeremy's eye. He pointed the light at the glass of water next to his bed. "Look at this!" he said. The water in the glass was filled with ripples.

They gathered around the glass.

"So what's the big deal?" Trent demanded.

Dean looked closely at the rippling water. "What could cause that?" he asked.

"I read somewhere that when a castle was under siege," Jeremy said, "the defenders would place a bowl of water on the floor to detect tunneling by their enemies. The water would ripple in response to the vibrations caused by the digging. Water doesn't move by itself. Something is making it move."

"Aw," Trent said, "you guys are screwy."

"Shhh," Dean said. "Listen!"

They all listened carefully.

"What is that sound?" Dean asked, whispering.

"I don't hear anything," Trent responded.

"Listen!" Dean said again.

Now they could hear a faint sound of metal clanking.

"I hear it," Trent said. "It's probably Percival cleaning all that armor. Let's go back to bed."

Dean got down on his hands and knees and placed his ear to the floor. "It's coming from somewhere downstairs," he said.

The clanking paused and then there was a loud clatter of pieces of metal crashing together.

"I think we'd better take a look," Dean said, putting on his sneakers.

Trent pulled on his sneakers. "Let me go first," he said, pushing past the others toward the door.

"I thought he wanted to go back to sleep," Jeremy said to Dean.

"So now our fearless leader is curious," Dean replied as they followed Trent into the dark hall.

CHAPTER
12

"Who's that?" someone whispered hoarsely in the dark hallway.

"Wha . . ." Trent bellowed in surprise, stopping short.

The beam of Jeremy's flashlight picked out Kari and Donna crouching near the wall.

"Where'd you come from?" Dean blurted out.

"Whoa, you really scared us," Kari said, straightening up. "What are you doing here?"

"We asked first," Trent snapped.

"Something woke us up," Kari said. "I heard somebody calling Elaine's name."

"Me, too," Donna agreed.

"I thought I was dreaming," Kari continued, "but then I realized I was awake."

"Yeah," Donna added, "so did I. But whoever heard of two people having the same dream at the same time?"

"Maybe somebody *was* calling her," Dean remarked. "Maybe this castle has an intercom or something."

"Or maybe it was magic!" Trent said sarcastically.

"Something woke us up, too," Jeremy said. "We heard a strange clanging sound and then we heard a crash downstairs."

"I heard strange sounds coming from downstairs, too," Kari said, looking at Donna.

Donna nodded in agreement. "I thought it might be an earthquake. We have a lot of quakes back home. I got right out of bed, put on my shoes, and went to find Kari. They taught us in school that the best thing you can do is get to a doorway or someplace sturdy. This old castle is pretty rickety."

"Rickety?" Trent said in disbelief. "This place is made of solid stone."

"A pile of stones can fall down, too, you know," Donna said defensively.

"Donna got me and we ran to Elaine's room," Kari continued, ignoring Trent, "but Elaine isn't there. The room is empty!"

"We were just going to look for her," Donna

said. "My hair dryer's gone and I think she took it."

"My radio is missing, too," Dean complained.

"Why would Elaine steal a hair dryer?" Jeremy wondered out loud.

"I'll bet she's up to something," Trent suggested. "She's probably laughing at us right now."

"Let's find out," Kari said.

"Yeah," Trent said. "C'mon, follow me."

Kari shrugged. "Who made him leader?" she asked in a low voice. Then she and the others followed Trent downstairs.

At the bottom of the stairs Trent turned and entered the Great Hall. But it was empty, lit only by the dying fire in the huge fireplace.

"Nothing here," Trent announced.

Jeremy swept his flashlight around the room. "No sign of Elaine," he said.

"Do that again," Kari said.

"Do what?" Jeremy asked.

"Shine the light around."

Jeremy slowly swept the light along the walls of the Great Hall. The swords and spears on the walls glimmered, but the room was empty.

"Let's try the library," Trent said.

"Wait a minute," Kari broke in. "Something's different."

"I don't see any . . ." Trent started to say.

"You're right!" Jeremy interrupted. "Something *has* changed."

"It's just the dark," Trent said with a sneer.

"No, it's not!" Jeremy said. "Look at the walls. All the suits of armor are missing!"

"What do you mean?" Trent asked.

"Look!" Donna said, pointing.

It was true. All the suits of armor that had lined the walls of the Great Hall were gone. Only footprints in the dust showed where they had stood.

"What is going on here?" Dean asked. "First Trent's watch and my radio disappear, then Donna's hair dryer, and now all these statues."

"They weren't statues," Jeremy said. "They were the kind of armor knights used to wear."

"I know, I know," Dean replied, "but why are they all missing?"

"Hey," Kari said. "Listen."

The clattering noise of metal scraping they had heard upstairs had started again, although now it was much louder.

"It's coming from below us," Kari said. "There must be a basement."

"Or a dungeon," added Jeremy.

CHAPTER
13

They looked around the Great Hall, searching for a doorway that would lead them down to the basement, but they couldn't find one.

"Maybe there's a way down in the library," Dean suggested. "That weird lady we saw might have been going downstairs."

They all went into the library and began searching for a door.

"I'm sure she went through here," Kari said, feeling her way along the wall. There wasn't any opening in the solid stone wall.

Jeremy poked around the desk where Professor Emrys had been sitting, looking at the piles of books. There were dozens of sheets of heavy paper covered with a strange spidery handwriting. Some of the letters looked familiar, but he couldn't quite make out the words. It reminded him of some of the old manuscripts he had seen in the British Museum.

There were also drawings of moths and butterflies, but they were mixed with plans for machinery and strange charts with weird symbols, stars and moons, and mathematical signs. Jeremy held up one sheet. Patterns of color on the paper seemed to move, dancing and shifting hypnotically. He put the paper down and rubbed his eyes. "This doesn't make any sense at all," he said, shaking his head.

"Of course not," Trent said sharply from over near the fireplace. "Do you think you're smart enough to understand some old weird professor's writings?"

Dean came over and inspected the papers. "Jeremy's right," he said after a moment. "This stuff is too mixed up to make any sense. It's like the professor is trying to bring together different things that shouldn't be mixed."

"Yeah, right," Trent said, leaning against one of the great iron supports that held up the huge mantle over the fireplace. "Like you'd know what that old coot is studying, too."

With a great scraping sound, the iron bracket suddenly shifted under Trent's weight, throwing him off balance and onto the floor.

A stone door just inside the fireplace slowly swung open, revealing a dark passageway.

Jeremy rushed over and peered inside. "I should have guessed," he said. "Many castles had secret passages for people to escape trouble. No invader would try to get past a roaring fire."

Trent stood up and pushed Jeremy aside. He started to go through the doorway then hesitated and turned back. "Donna and Kari," he said, "you stay here . . . where it's safe."

"No way you're leaving me behind!" Donna replied firmly.

"Give me the flashlight," Kari added. "I'll go first if you're afraid."

Kari grabbed the flashlight and ducked through the secret doorway into the stone passageway. Its ceiling was too low to stand up straight.

The others quickly followed, with Trent going last. As he stepped through, there was a low rumble and the door swung shut behind him.

"Hey!" Trent shouted. He banged on the stone door with his fist.

The others turned. Kari shined the flashlight around the door. There were no levers or latches or other way to open it. The dark passageway was the only way out.

CHAPTER
14

"If this is another one of Elaine's tricks . . ." Trent sputtered, pounding on the stone door.

". . . like the one she played in the Tower," Jeremy completed Trent's sentence.

"You can beat on that door all you want," Kari said. "All you're going to do is hurt your fist. C'mon. This passage is the only way out."

The passage had a musty smell and cobwebs hung from its ceiling, but after a few steps they could straighten up as they walked. Donna covered her hair with her hands.

Kari's light revealed a stone staircase, spiraling down into the blackness. "I guess we'd better follow it down," Kari said uncertainly.

"It will probably take us down into the castle

dungeons," Jeremy said. "There has to be another way out from there."

They followed the spiral stairway downward, turning to the right in tight circles. Kari's flashlight could only reach a few steps at a time. Everyone else had to feel their way around the spiral in the dark.

"This was on my list of things to see," Jeremy told them. "Spiral staircases in castles turn counterclockwise, so defenders can retreat up the stairs while swinging their swords with their right hand. An attacker had to lean around the corner to use his sword."

"Save it, Jeremy!" Trent said in disgust.

"There's light ahead," Donna said hopefully. "We're saved!"

"Shush, all of you," Dean replied. "I hear something."

There was light coming from below them, but now they could hear the rasping and clanking sounds they had heard before, the sound of metal scraping against metal.

"What is it?" Kari asked, whispering.

There was a loud crash!

The teens stopped short on the stairs. There was silence for a moment, and then the metallic clanking began again, but this time it seemed to be farther away.

"What is it?" Donna asked this time.

"I don't know," Dean responded, "but it seems to be moving away."

"Come on," Kari said. "Let's find out." She quickly led the way down the few remaining stairs and through an arched doorway into a dimly lit room.

They paused. The room was a jumble of gray stone arches and shadows that seemed to stretch as far as they could see. The air was very chilly and smelled musty and stale. A small fire burned on a metal grill in a stone circle in front of them, but the light seemed to come from all around them. The wall opposite them was lined with wooden doors. Scattered around the floor were strange mechanisms made of metal and wood.

Jeremy was excited. "This is the real thing," he said, "a real dungeon. Just like I've read about."

Donna shivered. "This is scary."

Jeremy walked around one of the devices. "Look here. A real rack. See how much heavier it is than the one in the Tower of London." He pulled on one of the heavy ropes. "You couldn't break these."

"Maybe I can get some light down here by clapping," Trent said, raising his hands.

"No, no," Dean spoke up. "You might turn these lights off. Don't clap!"

"Wow!" Jeremy said, moving to a large wooden table. "Look here. Thumbscrews, an iron boot— they've got everything!" But the things on the table were covered with cobwebs and dust. "They haven't been used in a long time," Jeremy remarked.

"I hope they were never used," Donna responded.

"Okay, enough!" Dean said. "We're here to find Elaine, not to check out torture instruments."

Jeremy sheepishly came back to the group.

"What do we do now?" Kari asked.

"C'mon," Dean said. "Let's check this place out. Elaine's got to be around here somewhere. Try some of those doors." He pointed across the room.

They tried the doors, but they were securely bolted with chains and large rusty padlocks. Trent pulled on a lock experimentally, but it didn't give.

"Well, where do we go now?" Kari asked.

Dean held up his hand. "Listen!"

There was a clanking sound. It sounded like footsteps. And it was coming nearer.

"It sounds like the Tin Woodsman to me," Donna whispered.

The clanking was louder. The noise echoed in the dungeon.

"Hide!" Kari said urgently.

They scattered into the shadows. Kari and Trent

hid behind an arch. Jeremy ducked under the rack, and Donna and Dean crouched behind the wooden table.

There was a crashing noise and a figure dressed in armor stepped down the stairs and through the arch they had entered from. The visor of the helmet was closed, hiding the face inside.

The knight marched steadily across the dungeon to one of the locked doors, his footsteps resounding loudly off the stone walls.

The knight reached out with his left hand and pulled on the hinges of the door. With a loud squeak, the door slowly opened, but it opened backward. It swung on its latched side, supported by the rusty lock.

The figure in armor entered and the door slammed shut behind him.

CHAPTER
15

"What was that?" Donna asked, standing up behind the table.

"Somebody dressed up for a masquerade," Trent replied, going over to the door the knight had just gone through.

"What did he look like?" Jeremy asked, crawling out from under the rack. He was covered with cobwebs and dust. "I could only see his legs."

Kari went over to Jeremy and helped him dust himself off. "It looked like some weirdo wearing one of those suits of armor that used to be upstairs. We couldn't see his face."

"Maybe it was Percival," Donna suggested.

Trent was trying to open the door, but he could

barely move it. "Give me a hand," he said, turning to the others.

"You're not seriously planning on going in there, are you?" Dean asked.

"How else are we going to find Elaine?" Kari replied.

"She's right," Jeremy agreed. He went over to Trent and tried to help pull the door open. The others quickly joined them.

"If we all pull together," Dean said, "we ought to be able to move it."

They pulled hard and slowly the door began to move. Then it seemed to give way and swung wide.

"Quick!" Kari said. "Get in."

They slipped through the doorway and into the passage beyond. The door swung shut behind them with a bang.

"That guy must be really strong," Kari remarked.

"Knights had to be," Jeremy replied, rubbing one arm. "They had to be able to fight with all that armor on. It could weigh a hundred pounds or more."

The passageway behind the door was narrow, but it was also lit by a strange glimmering light.

Trent led the way as they all moved slowly along the passage.

"Hey," Donna said, "it's sloping downhill. Is there anything lower than a dungeon?"

"Not that I know of," Jeremy answered.

"That's a first," Trent remarked.

"This is no time to be mean, Trent," Kari said.

The passage wound downward for several hundred feet and then stopped abruptly at the top of another spiral stairway. They could clearly hear the sound of metal clanking below them.

"I guess we follow," Dean said doubtfully.

Suddenly a freezing blast of air swept up the stairs.

"What was that?" Kari asked.

"Something's going on below," Trent declared.

They started down the spiral stairs, but Jeremy paused. "Wait a minute," he said. "A breeze like that could only be caused by someone opening the door we just came through. Someone's behind us!"

CHAPTER
16

Everyone was moving down the stairs as quickly as they could, almost running. But they had to step carefully because the stone stairs were old and worn. Their narrow, uneven surfaces were slippery and they were cut at odd angles to make the spiral.

Donna's feet slipped out from under her and she sat down hard with an "ow!"

Dean stopped and leaned back to give her a hand. Something rumbled loudly and suddenly he was down, too.

The stairs were moving! They were snaking downward like some sort of escalator, spinning in a tight circle. The others tried to stay on their feet, but the revolving stairs sent them sprawling. The rumbling was getting louder. The stairs were whirling faster!

"What's happening?" Dean shouted.

The noise was so loud he couldn't hear an answer, if there was one.

The stairs were spinning at a dizzying speed. Everyone held on, trying not to slip off as they were carried downward. The stone walls of the stairwell blurred as they slid past them.

Suddenly the grinding rumble of the stairs softened. The stairs slowed, then stopped abruptly. They tried to hold on, but their momentum carried them forward, sliding down the remaining stairs and through a doorway at the bottom. They landed together, sprawling in a heap.

They slowly stood. Trent rubbed his knee where it had hit the floor. Donna straightened her clothes. Jeremy shook his head from side to side, trying to get rid of his dizziness.

"Everyone okay?" Kari asked.

"Yeah," Dean replied, "but I don't want to go on that roller coaster again."

"Where are we now, genius?" Trent asked Jeremy.

"It's some sort of cave," Jeremy responded, looking around.

The walls and ceiling were glistening white in

the pale light. Several thick white columns rose from the floor to the ceiling. The columns were surrounded by hundreds of stalactites hanging down, looking like icicles.

Trent touched the nearest wall. "It's made of ice," he said, pulling his hand back quickly.

They couldn't tell how large the cave was, but it seemed huge, fading into dark shadows in the distance. A large pool of frozen water reflected the white walls and ceiling. But ahead of them, in the center of the cave, was the most surprising thing of all. It was their minivan, parked with its headlights on.

"How'd that get here?" Dean whispered.

"Look there," Kari responded.

The van's headlights were pointed toward the far wall where several figures were working. They were digging a hole in the ice wall with picks and shovels. The headlights glinted off the figures. They looked like knights, dressed in full suits of dull gray armor, their faces concealed by their helmets.

"Boy," Trent said loudly, "is this weird."

Dean shushed him and pulled him into the shadows with the others. The figures digging didn't seem to notice the noise, however. They were working very steadily, methodically swinging their picks and shovels in an almost mechanical manner. Their armor clanked and rattled as they worked. The hole in the wall of ice grew larger, big enough to hold a person.

A new noise in the shadows off to the right caught the teens' attention. There was a bright flash and suddenly Lady Viviane, the woman they had seen upstairs, emerged from the shadows. But she wasn't the same dreamy person they had seen in the library. She was wearing a black gown now and a black veil that covered her face. Her long dress swept the floor of the cave. She was full of energy and authority. She quickly strode over to where the knights were digging.

"Fast-er, fast-er, fast-er," she chanted, waving her hand in an intricate pattern in the air.

The knights in armor began to dig faster, making even more noise.

There was another flash, and a second figure suddenly materialized out of the shadows.

Donna gasped.

It was Elaine!

CHAPTER
17

It was Elaine all right, but it was a very different Elaine. She was dressed in a long gown made of some sort of sparkling green material that shimmered, even in the dim light of the ice cave. Her hair was pulled back and she wore a tiara, which also sparkled. But she seemed dazed, moving as though she were in some sort of dream.

Lady Viviane took Elaine by the hand and led her over to the side of the van. Elaine did exactly what Viviane wanted.

"It's like she's sleepwalking," Kari whispered.

"We've got to get her out of here," Dean said.

"We've got to get ourselves out of here," Trent said vehemently.

Viviane waved her hands. The knights in armor stopped digging, and the cave became quiet.

She stepped forward and examined their work. The hole in the ice was a square box, large enough to hold a person. It looked like a coffin!

Viviane motioned to Elaine. Elaine walked slowly from the van to the hole in the ice.

"Oh, my gosh!" Kari whispered. "She's going to put Elaine in that hole!"

Viviane laughed wickedly, putting her hand on Elaine's shoulder. "With your help, this will hold him for another thousand years," she said.

"I don't think so!" A strong voice came from the other side of the cave. Professor Emrys stepped out of the shadows. But he too was very different from the person they had seen upstairs. He seemed taller and more powerful, and his white beard sparkled. He wore a long purple robe and a tall pointed hat with strange designs on it.

"Emrys . . . I knew I recognized that name," Jeremy murmured. "It's Merlin!"

"Who?" Kari whispered in disbelief.

"Merlin!" Jeremy replied.

"Release the girl and I shan't be hard on you this time, Viviane," Emrys demanded, his voice echoing in the cave.

Viviane spun around. Her veil fell away from her

face, revealing it. Her features were sharp and her blonde hair had streaks of white. She grinned hideously. "She is mine, Merlin," she sneered. "Her power is mine! You're finished. Forever!"

Viviane uttered something rapidly, and blue sparks flew upward from her hands. With a loud crack, a large chunk of ice sheared off the ceiling and fell toward Merlin.

Merlin made a small gesture with his right hand, so small it looked almost casual. The piece of ice shattered in the air, spraying the walls harmlessly and splattering the teens where they hid.

Merlin and Viviane both began chanting rapidly and blue sparks flew from their hands. Cascades of sparks met between them, forming a flashing yellow and green ball of energy. The ball flared and grew, glowing brightly. It moved slowly back and forth between them. Each of them struggled, throwing more energy into the ball, but neither seemed able to gain the advantage.

"Look!" Trent exclaimed. "He's wearing my digital watch."

Merlin glanced in their direction but swiftly turned his attention back to Viviane.

That split second was all she needed. Viviane stepped behind Elaine, using her as a shield. "Stop, Merlin!" she commanded, placing both her hands on Elaine's shoulders. "Stop or I will cast a spell on this girl that will plague all of humankind!"

Merlin's hands stopped moving.

"Unless you do as I say," Viviane threatened, "I will use the Charm of Nothtoad and poison the world."

Merlin seemed to wilt, dropping his arms to his sides. "You would, wouldn't you, Viviane," he said. "You know I cannot let the innocent be harmed."

"You know where you belong," Viviane said haughtily, nodding toward the hole in the ice wall. "My knights have prepared a new home for you. It's better than the last cell I buried you in. This one will keep you for even more than a thousand years."

Merlin now seemed old and weak. His body bent over as he shuffled toward the ice cell. He shook his head weakly from side to side, and for a moment it looked like he glanced at the teens hidden in the shadows.

"Get in," Viviane ordered.

Merlin stepped into the cell in the ice. Viviane waved her hands and ice flowed magically over the hole, sealing it. She made another gesture and the knights in armor began packing more ice against the hole, until a large pile covered its entrance.

In a few moments it was done. Merlin was trapped in an ice prison.

Viviane laughed in triumph. Then she led Elaine and the knights into the shadows and out of sight. Their noise slowly died away.

The teens stepped out of the shadows. The lights of the minivan were still on and they could just make out the figure of Merlin in his purple robe through the layers of ice.

"What do we do now?" Donna cried.

CHAPTER
18

"We've got to rescue Elaine," Kari said decisively.

They stood together near the entrance to the ice cavern, its silent white walls stretching around them.

"Maybe we can use the van to get out of here," Dean suggested.

"And who's going to drive it?" Trent asked sarcastically. "You?"

Dean shook his head. "There doesn't seem to be a way to drive it out of here anyway."

"We've got to follow that lady and her knights and rescue Elaine," Kari insisted.

"But what about the old guy in the ice?" Trent asked.

"You mean Merlin," Jeremy answered.

Trent spun toward Jeremy. "How do you know he's Merlin, genius?"

"It has to be Merlin," Jeremy said. "Emrys was Merlin's name as a boy."

"And that's what that mean old lady called him," Donna chimed in.

"It's all legend, of course," Jeremy said thoughtfully.

"You mean it's all just made up," Trent said.

"Merlin . . . King Arthur . . . The Knights of the Round Table?" Dean asked doubtfully. "You mean all that stuff?"

Jeremy shrugged. "It could be made up, I guess."

"Maybe Merlin can help us save Elaine," Kari suggested. "We should get him out of the ice."

"That won't be necessary," came a deep voice from behind them.

They whirled around toward the sound of the voice. A huge knight stood in the doorway to the spiral stairs. His armor was brightly polished, shining silver in the dim light of the cave. In his right hand he carried a broadsword that was almost as tall as he was. The knight's helmet was topped by a scarlet plume and its visor was raised.

Kari recognized the knight. "It's Percival," she said, with a quick sigh of relief.

Percival strode over to them, holding his

broadsword high. "Emrys will get out on his own," he said. "He always does. All we can do is wait."

The teens all started to speak at once. Finally Dean asked, "Please tell us what's going on here."

Percival glanced at the figure in the ice. "This is part of a long battle. The Master and Lady Viviane have been enemies for many years."

"You mean many *centuries*, don't you?" Jeremy interjected.

Percival looked Jeremy up and down. "You have guessed, I see," he said. "Not many visitors have reasoned out what is happening here."

"You have a lot of visitors?" Donna asked.

"Not so many at one time. Your group is very unusual. But one or two guests have appeared every now and then."

"What about Elaine?" Kari asked.

"Oh, she's comparatively safe for now," Percival replied. "Lady Viviane needs your friend's power. She won't do anything to jeopardize that . . . unless. . ."

"Unless what?" Donna asked quickly.

Percival paused and looked at each of the teens. "I think I had better go back to the beginning." He placed the broadsword pointing downward in front of him and put both hands on its hilt. "You have guessed who my master is. He is Merlin, the great magician and councilor to King Arthur. Viviane was one of the people who tried to stop Arthur. She worked with the evil sorceress, Morgan le Fay, to destroy the Round Table and all it stood for. Viviane's task was to neutralize Merlin. This she did, and she did it very well indeed."

"Wait a minute," Trent interrupted. "You think we're going to believe all this baloney?"

Percival glared at Trent. "Frankly, young man, I don't care what you believe. Chivalry demands that I speak the truth. This is the truth."

Trent drew back sullenly.

"Viviane tricked Merlin into believing that she loved him. She beguiled him and got him to tell her all his secrets. He taught her his magic, how to make potions and talismans and amulets. He taught her how to assume the shapes of animals and how to read dreams. . . ."

"Animals?" Jeremy interrupted. "Like a mouse?"

Percival nodded and continued his story. "Viviane stayed with Merlin for years, working in this castle, learning all she could. She was a dangerous trickster, an enchantress . . ." Percival's voice trailed off.

"And then what happened?" Donna asked.

"One day word came to Viviane from Morgan le Fay. Arthur had been sick and the kingdom was weak. The Knights of the Round Table had scattered, searching for the Holy Grail. It was time to strike! Morgan le Fay's armies were on the march and Viviane was prepared to defeat Merlin. She tricked him into coming down here and she cast a spell, sealing him in the ice. She imprisoned him and froze this whole cave. Then she prepared to join Morgan le Fay and defeat King Arthur.

"But Merlin was more clever than she supposed. While she was trapping him here, he trapped her in the castle above. Magic takes great strength. It drains a person. When Viviane was finished sealing Merlin in the ice cave, she was too weak to break the charms he had created to seal the castle from prying eyes. Viviane went into a terrible rage, trying to break through. She tried everything she had been taught, but nothing worked. And casting spells just made her weaker. Viviane was just as trapped as Merlin was!"

"But she has power now," Kari said.

"Yes," Percival agreed, "but Merlin's power is still greater. He slept in the ice and when he awoke, he broke free. But he still loves Viviane and can't bring himself to punish her. Keeping her trapped in this castle is as far as he will go. He keeps the castle invisible to all outsiders and he keeps Viviane trapped inside."

"But we saw the castle. What happened this time?" Jeremy asked.

Percival frowned. "Merlin is the keeper of the land. The land has always been the source of his strength. That is why the Lady of the Lake entrusted him with Excalibur, the great sword of King Arthur. It is the symbol of the power to heal the land and bring its people together. While Merlin sleeps, he is restoring his powers. But now he has been awakened from his sleep by a threat to the land. There is devastation and ruin outside, what you call industrial pollution. The sky is dark and the air is hard to breath. Even the moths have changed color. Did none of your people notice anything?"

"He showed us a black moth upstairs," Dean said. "Does that have something to do with this?"

"Yes," Percival responded. "Whenever the land is in danger, Merlin awakes to try to do something about it. But Merlin cannot leave this castle. If he does, Viviane will escape, and her evil and mischief are great dangers to the world, perhaps even greater than the pollution. At least people like you can help clean up the air."

"But what does that have to do with Elaine?" Donna asked.

"Perhaps your friend is a bit of an enchantress herself." Percival suggested. "Does she enjoy playing tricks on people?"

"She sure does," Trent grimaced.

"I thought so," Percival continued. "Viviane needs someone whose energy is aligned with hers. It doesn't necessarily mean that person is bad. They just have to like tricking people. Viviane needs to steal power from a young woman to try to break free from Merlin's castle. And the young woman she has chosen is your friend Elaine."

CHAPTER
19

"But who are you?" Donna asked Percival.

Before Percival could answer, Jeremy spoke up. "I know who you are. You're the *real* Sir Percival, aren't you?"

Percival nodded. "Aye, that I am."

"But who *is* the real Percival?" Donna demanded.

"Percival was one of the Knights of the Round Table," Jeremy answered. "He was with King Arthur when he died."

"Whoa!" Trent exclaimed. "Where'd you get that? King Arthur is a myth. And if he was real, this guy would be hundreds of years old!"

"Let me explain," Percival continued, without a glance at Trent. "Lacking Merlin's help, Arthur was weakened, but when the word spread that Morgan le Fay was going to fight him, he was rejoined by many of the Knights of the Round Table, including Lancelot. The battle was waged in a thick mist. Many were killed. Even though his army was outnumbered, Arthur still managed to win. But he was mortally wounded in the battle.

"After the battle, he gave me Excalibur, his magic sword, and bade me throw it into the water. At first I refused. The sword meant too much to be thrown away. But Arthur ordered me to do it. I threw it as far as I could, and suddenly an arm appeared out of the water. It was the Lady of the Lake who had given Arthur the sword in the first place. She caught Excalibur in her hand and took it down into the deep. When I returned and reported what happened, Arthur seemed pleased. Then he boarded a boat, disappearing to the magical isle of Avalon."

"But like Trent said," Kari responded in amazement, "all that stuff with King Arthur happened a zillion years ago. How can you be alive?"

"How did you get here?" Jeremy asked. "You aren't magic, are you?"

"No, but the castle is magic," Percival replied. "Time in this castle is different from time outside. It moves slower. Sometimes it doesn't seem to move at all."

"But what happens here?" Jeremy asked. "I mean, what do you do?"

"I wait for Merlin. That is my duty."

"But I thought you said Merlin sleeps most of the time," Donna commented.

"He has awakened several times in the past," Percival replied, "but the land seemed safe enough, so he could go to sleep again, building his powers to defeat Viviane. But this time it is different. The land is in the worst shape he has ever seen it. You have done things that even Merlin could not imagine. You have spoiled the waters and killed the fishes. You have cut down the forests and leveled the hills."

"And that is what Merlin was trying to figure out in the library?" Dean asked.

"Yes," Percival answered. "That is why he let you find this castle, too. He wanted to see what manner of people would behave this way. He wanted to know more about your equipment and your way of living. He could not understand why you would treat the earth so badly. And you people have strange devices that Merlin doesn't understand," he said, pointing toward the minivan sitting with its lights on.

"Like my digital watch," Trent remarked.

Percival nodded.

"What's that noise?" Kari asked.

They heard a soft whirring sound from near the ice cell that held Merlin.

"What's going on?" Dean asked. "I think I saw him move."

"It's just the light playing tricks," Trent said.

"Don't be too sure," Jeremy said. "Look at that."

They could clearly see the figure inside the ice moving. The ice was turning from white to bright colors. The colors moved rapidly, arching like a rainbow, shimmering in red, green, yellow, and blue. Then the ice became transparent, like a pane of glass. They could see Merlin moving inside, but his image was blurred and wavering like a mirage.

The rainbow colors seemed to fold together into a glowing red point inside the ice. Merlin was pointing something at the ice and waving it in widening circles. They could see that the ice was melting now. A small stream of water flowed down the wall and along the floor to the frozen pond. The small stream swiftly became a flood.

A hole appeared in the ice and grew rapidly. Soon the hole was large enough and Merlin stepped out of his ice prison.

Merlin seemed to sag a little as he came out of the hole. He looked tired. Percival stepped toward him, but Merlin waved him away. Merlin took a deep breath. "There," he said, "that's much better." He stood up straight, once again looking tall and powerful.

Merlin held up the device that had helped him escape the ice. "You know," he said, "some of your inventions are really quite remarkable."

"That's my hair dryer!" Donna exclaimed.

CHAPTER
20

"Are you all right, Sire?" Percival asked.

Merlin nodded. "We have no time to lose. We've got to get that girl away from Lady Viviane. No telling what sort of calamity she's planning."

"But what about our visitors, Sire?" Percival asked.

Merlin surveyed the teens. "We can use their help, if they are willing," he said. "Remember, Viviane's forces outnumber us."

Percival turned toward the teens. "Are you willing then?"

There was no hesitation. They all shouted, "Yes!"

"We must get upstairs as quickly as possible," Merlin said. "Whatever Viviane's planning, she first has to break free of the castle. The dungeon is the weak point in the spell that keeps her here. No doubt she knows that. But the real exit is in the Great Hall." He paused in thought for a moment. "No doubt she knows that, too," he mused.

Percival agreed. "We'll go up by the spiral staircase, Sire."

"Then I will take my own special route," Merlin responded. "I will meet you upstairs in the Great Hall. Watch for her knights. They could be anywhere."

Merlin spun away from them and lifted his arms. His purple cloak spread wide, momentarily hiding him. The cloak suddenly glowed yellow, then vanished in a cloud of smoke.

"Awesome!" Dean exclaimed. "He disappeared."

"No he didn't," Jeremy responded. "That's him."

He pointed to a small brown mouse that sat where Merlin had been. The mouse turned around and stared at the teens. It had a white muzzle and bright black eyes.

"That's the mouse I saw upstairs," Trent said in surprise.

"You mean it's the one you threw a pillow at," Dean reminded him.

The brown mouse bowed toward them, then turned and scampered away into the shadows.

Percival looked at the teens. "Are you ready?" he asked.

The teens nodded.

"Then follow me," Percival said, lifting his broadsword. He led the way to the entrance of the spiral staircase. The staircase looked steep and narrow in the dark shadows.

"Ugh!" Donna said. "Are we going to have to climb all those stairs?"

"No telling how many there are," Kari said. "We didn't exactly count them on the way down."

"We didn't even step on most of them on the way down," Jeremy added.

Percival moved onto the stairs. "Come along," he said. "We've not time to waste."

Dean and Jeremy entered the stairway behind Percival, with Kari and Trent close behind.

"C'mon, Donna," Kari called back.

Donna hesitated, but then realized that she was all alone in the ice cavern. She quickly caught up with them.

They heard a familiar rumble and the stairs began moving again, but this time they were moving upward.

The rumble turned into a roar in the darkness.

The walls became a blur in the beam of Kari's flashlight. They were moving so fast, their ears popped.

"Hold on!" Kari shouted above the roar. "It's going to stop quick."

But this time the stairs did not stop abruptly. Instead, the roar began to diminish, and the stairs slowed, gradually coming to a stop.

"Quiet, now," Percival whispered. "They will try to surprise us."

They followed Percival closely as he led the way up the last few steps and into the passageway above. He cracked the door open and peered through. Then, lifting his broadsword, he stepped into the dimly lit dungeon. The others followed closely.

"Look out!" Percival shouted.

Arrayed in a half circle, Viviane's army of knights waited for them with drawn weapons, their faces concealed by their closed visors. Their gray armor made them look like shadows in the faint light.

Without warning, the door to the spiral staircase slammed shut.

Percival lowered his visor and swung his sword in front of him.

With a growling sound, all of Viviane's knights advanced.

CHAPTER
21

Holding his heavy broadsword with both hands, Percival attacked the nearest knight. The knight swung at Percival's head with a heavy mace. Just in time, Percival parried the blow, his sword clanging loudly as it struck the mace, cutting it in half.

Percival swung again. His sword struck deep into the armor covering the knight's shoulder. The knight didn't seem to notice. It just kept swinging mechanically with the broken mace.

Viviane's other knights closed in and began hacking at Percival. They moved very deliberately, just as they had when they were digging in the ice. The sound of clashing metal echoed in the dungeon.

Percival parried and struck as quickly as he could. He was faster than Viviane's knights were, but they slowly forced him back toward the door-way, where the teens were huddled.

"There are too many of them!" Trent shouted.

A sword slammed into Percival's armor, but he kept his footing.

"We've got to help him," Kari added.

"How?" Dean asked, drawing back from the rag-ing battle.

Jeremy looked around for something that could help. He spied a battle-ax leaning against the wall a short distance away. He moved quickly to get it.

Percival was now in the center of a circle of Viviane's knights, all of them trying to slash him. He spun and thrust his sword, parrying their blows. He still moved much faster than they did, but Viviane's knights were wearing him down.

Jeremy reached the battle-ax and grabbed its long wooden handle.

One of Viviane's knights turned toward Jeremy. Jeremy pulled on the battle-ax's handle. The knight ran toward him, swinging his sword.

The battle-ax was too heavy! As Jeremy pulled on it, he slipped and fell.

The knight clattered toward him. Jeremy closed his eyes tightly, expecting a blow from the knight's sword.

The knight's foot struck Jeremy hard instead

and there was a loud clatter. Carried along by the force of its charge, the knight had tripped, tumbling over Jeremy and crashing to the stone floor.

Jeremy opened his eyes. The knight's armor had struck the stones and fallen to pieces. Parts of it were scattered all across the floor.

The suit of armor was empty!

Jeremy thought quickly. "It's magic!" he cried out. "They're not real!"

Trent saw what had happened to Jeremy. "I can handle these guys," he said to himself. He rushed forward to where Percival was fighting and tackled one of the knights from behind. The suit of armor fell forward and seemed almost to explode as it hit the floor.

Trent slowly stood up. "That armor is harder than it looks," he said ruefully, rubbing his bruised shoulder.

Dean picked up a wooden bucket from the floor and swung it as hard as he could, striking another suit of armor. An arm clattered to the floor, but the knight didn't seem to notice. It turned menacingly toward Dean. Dean retreated as the one-armed knight advanced. The knight lifted its sword to strike!

Suddenly the knight's helmet flew off. The suit of armor collapsed in a heap, revealing Kari standing behind. She was holding the flashlight, now broken into two pieces.

Another knight went for Donna where she crouched by the wall. She dodged to the side and the knight's sword clanged against the stones.

Jeremy stood up and grabbed the battle-ax again. "How about some help?" he shouted.

Dean hurried over to him and together they lifted the heavy battle-ax.

"C'mon," Jeremy said. They rushed at the knight attacking Donna, carrying the battle-ax between them. The handle caught the knight behind the knees and the suit of armor tipped over, falling to pieces as it struck the floor.

Now that the odds were more even, Percival was gaining the advantage. His great sword cut through the suits of armor, scattering pieces about the dungeon. The noise of the growling had diminished with the collapse of each of Viviane's knights, but the other knights didn't seem to notice. There were only a few left, but they still kept coming.

Trent threw a block on another knight and it clattered to the ground.

With a final sweep of his great sword, Percival knocked the helmet off the last knight and the suit of armor slowly toppled over with a final crash.

The dungeon was quiet.

The teens gathered around Percival. Kari stood next to Dean. He smiled at her. "Sorry about the flashlight," he said.

"Better tell that to Jeremy," Kari replied. "It was his flashlight."

Percival pushed up his visor and looked around the dungeon at the scattered armor. "Thank you, lads and lassies," he said. "Merlin said you could help me if you were willing. I couldn't have done it without your aid. This was a nice night's work."

Trent groaned. "What a lousy pun."

"No pun intended," Percival said seriously. "Now we've got to find your friend."

CHAPTER
22

Percival led the way upstairs to the Great Hall. This time they went by the main stairway.

Lady Viviane awaited them, standing next to the round table in the middle of the Great Hall. Her veil was back in place, covering her face and shoulders. A blue aura seemed to shimmer around her long gown and gather near her hands. A black curtain concealed the end of the Great Hall behind her.

"I've been expecting you," she said haughtily. "I'm surprised you took so long getting here."

"We had a little encounter downstairs," Percival replied.

"I hope you weren't too inconvenienced," Lady Viviane remarked. She laughed scornfully.

"Hardly at all," Percival replied. "Nothing my companions and I couldn't handle."

"We fixed your friends," Trent said.

"They're scattered all over the dungeon," Kari added.

"No matter," Lady Viviane replied. "I'll reassemble them later." She looked closely at the group. "Where is your tired old master?" she asked Percival.

"He's neither tired nor old," Percival said gallantly. "He'll be along in his own good time."

"Always in his own good time," Lady Viviane said. "Well, then, I have a little something to show you while we wait." She waved her right hand and the dark curtain behind her opened wide and then rose into the air.

Donna gasped.

Behind the curtain was a raised platform, its five steps carpeted with a fabric of reds and golds woven in an intricate pattern. On the platform was a large throne that shimmered with gold and precious stones, glowing in the light of the Great Hall. A figure was seated on the throne, dressed in a jeweled gown with a heavy golden crown. It was Elaine.

Kari moved forward, but Lady Viviane blocked her way.

"Tut, tut, my dear," Lady Viviane said. "Mustn't

bother her when she's having such a good time."

Elaine looked as though she was asleep with her eyes open, staring straight ahead. Her expression was vacant.

"What have you done to her?" Donna demanded. "She's our friend!"

"But she's *my* companion," Lady Viviane replied. "She will do whatever I say."

Kari tried to get around Lady Viviane. "Elaine!" she called. "Wake up!"

The sound of Kari's voice seemed to startle Elaine awake. She shifted uncomfortably and started to rise from the throne.

But Lady Viviane moved quickly to Elaine's side, gently pushing her back down. "You must stay where you are," Lady Viviane warned her. "Move and you will lose all that is promised to you. Stay and all the riches of the world will be yours." Her voice was soothing and hypnotic.

"We've got to stop her!" Dean said to the others.

They started to move toward the throne.

Viviane laughed scornfully. "Nothing can stop me now!" She waved her hands and a wall of orange light suddenly appeared in front of the teens.

Dean reached forward to touch the orange light. "Ow!" he said, jerking his hand back as sparks flew.

"Let that be a warning," Lady Viviane said.

"You are playing with powers you do not understand."

"Elaine!" Kari and Donna both called desperately. "Elaine! Wake up!"

Elaine heard her friends' voices and started to rise again.

Lady Viviane stepped away from the throne and mumbled some strange words very quickly. A green smoke began to seep out around her hands and flow toward the throne where Elaine sat. Elaine rose and started to step forward, but she slumped back down as the thick smoke billowed around her.

The smoke cloaked the throne, hiding it from view.

Jeremy caught sight of something else. A small brown mouse scampered out of nowhere and disappeared behind the throne as it was enveloped in the smoke.

Suddenly the green smoke began to move. Great puffs of smoke ballooned toward Lady Viviane. She screamed in rage and threw up her hands. Before the smoke could surround her, the shimmering barrier of orange light that had imprisoned the teens vanished and reappeared, surrounding Lady Viviane. The orange light seemed to suck the smoke up, absorbing it, causing both to disappear.

As the smoke whirled past, the teens caught

sight of Merlin, standing next to Elaine, waving his hand in a strange manner. The smoke cleared and they could make out what he was doing. He was blowing the smoke away with Donna's hair dryer.

But Lady Viviane wasn't finished yet. She rose to her full height and shouted some magic words. She seemed to grow larger as the room grew dark.

Suddenly a cold wind whooshed through the Great Hall. It whipped past the teens, then seemed to gather around Lady Viviane. Black storm clouds gathered above her head, appearing out of nowhere. The clouds billowed and collided. Bolts of lightning split the air, striking the ground around her. Thunder roared and the black clouds swirled and grew. A stream of air rushed upward around Lady Viviane, peeling away her veil and blowing her hair straight up.

"Look!" Donna cried. "Look how old she is!"

Lady Viviane's hair was now completely white. Her cheeks were sunken and her skin was heavily wrinkled. She threw back her head and laughed wickedly. Her laughter echoed in the Great Hall, mixing with the sound of the thunder.

The teens pulled back in fear, but Percival held his ground, keeping his sword ready.

"This is like a bad dream!" Donna exclaimed.

"He'll be fried if that lightning strikes his armor," Dean said.

"She's not after him," Kari replied. "She's after Merlin."

Lady Viviane suddenly spread her arms wide and turned slowly to face Merlin. Then she clapped her hands loudly and the thunder stopped. She pointed at Merlin and Elaine and chanted some sort of magical spell.

An arrow of ice leaped from the black cloud above Lady Viviane, hurtling toward Merlin and Elaine.

Merlin said something quickly and gestured with the hair dryer. Flame erupted from the hair dryer's nozzle, shooting toward Lady Viviane.

Ice and flame met in midair, boiling and fusing. There was a great hissing sound and a burst of white steam.

Merlin's flame was melting Lady Viviane's stream of ice into water and then boiling it. But Lady Viviane kept the ice flowing.

Both Merlin and Lady Viviane stood like statues, leaning rigidly toward each other. The cloud of steam billowed and hissed, slowly moving back and forth between Merlin and Lady Viviane as though each one were pushing against the other. But if one of the wizards seemed to be gaining the advantage, the other increased the effort and forced the ball of steam back. They chanted steadily, concentrating every effort on forcing the other back, but neither seemed to be able to dominate the other.

The Great Hall became damp and clammy as it slowly filled with steamy mist. The mist clung to the teens like sweat, and the air tasted of iron.

"What's that noise?" Donna asked.

The others heard it, too. Over the chanting of the wizards and the hissing of the steam, there was music coming from the far corner of the Great Hall. It was getting louder. It was hard rock!

The sound of guitars and drums filled the hall. The music was loud, pounding. And it got louder!

Lady Viviane glanced toward the source of the music.

That was enough. Lady Viviane lost her concentration. The flame broke through the stream of ice and struck the black clouds above her head. The clouds turned gray, then red, and finally evaporated. Steam gathered around Lady Viviane, and she disappeared in the thick, billowing vapor.

The flame stopped. Merlin lowered the hair dryer.

As the steam dispersed, they could see Lady Viviane collapsed on the floor.

CHAPTER
23

Elaine shook her head slowly and yawned widely. Then she caught sight of the teens standing behind Percival. Her eyebrows arched in surprise. "What are you guys doing?" she asked.

"What are *we* doing!" Trent responded. "What do you mean? You're the one who's all dressed up!"

Elaine looked down and seemed to notice what she was wearing for the first time. She was so surprised she stood up suddenly and stepped forward.

Donna and Kari bolted past Percival and rushed to meet Elaine as she stepped off platform.

"Are you okay?" Donna asked.

"Sure," Elaine answered vaguely. "What's up?"

"Are you for real, girl?" Kari asked.

"What do you mean?" Elaine asked innocently.

They were interrupted by a gentle sighing sound that came from behind Elaine. Everyone turned toward it. As they watched, the throne seemed to melt like wax, turning into an old wooden chair.

"What's that?" Donna shrieked, jumping away from Elaine.

Elaine's shimmering dress was undergoing the same change as the throne. It seemed to flow and melt, revealing Elaine's jeans and baggy denim shirt.

"Lady Viviane is a master of illusion," Merlin said, "but that's all it is—illusion."

Percival took a step toward Lady Viviane who still lay on the floor.

"Wait!" Merlin commanded. Percival halted.

A yellow glow seemed to gather around Lady Viviane, outlining her body on the floor, then covering all of her. Her outline began to waver and flow, just as the throne had.

"Come over here," Percival said to the girls, lifting his sword.

The girls pulled away from the wooden chair and joined the others behind Percival.

"What's going on?" Dean asked.

"She's collecting her energy," Percival said.

Lady Viviane's shape began to shrink, collapsing bit by bit as smoke rose around it. As she became smaller, the yellow glow became more intense.

Then there was a bright blue flash.

A black raven stood where Lady Viviane had been, smoke rising in a circle around it.

"I warned you!" the raven said in a harsh voice. "The curse of Nothtoad be upon you." Then the bird mumbled some phrases.

"A talking bird?" Dean said in disbelief.

"Yes, a talking bird," Percival said, "and if you want to stay alive, we'd better stop her from talking." He lunged with his sword at the raven.

The raven jumped and took flight. It flapped up to the ceiling, its wings laboring, and settled on one of the rafters.

"Too slow," the raven said. Then it cawed loudly. Its voice sounded like laughter.

They all stared up at the raven.

"Big deal," Trent said. "Who's afraid of a bird?"

"If Lady Viviane completes her curse," Percival responded anxiously, "we're done for!"

The raven stood on the rafter and preened its feathers. Then it spoke again. "Now to end this little game. The Curse of Nothtoad, I call . . ."

An owl appeared out of nowhere and swooped toward the raven. The raven jumped aside and plunged toward the floor. The owl banked quickly and followed the raven down. The raven began to shimmer with a purple light.

The shape of the raven was already changing when it landed on the floor. With a bright flash Lady Viviane reappeared.

The owl was shimmering, too. It landed quickly and, with a another flash, was replaced by Merlin.

The air around Lady Viviane shimmered, and she became a large black snake with long fangs.

The teens recoiled in fear.

The snake followed Merlin's movements, twisting and slithering as it prepared to strike. It reared its head back, its fangs dripping with venom. The snake struck, but hit only empty air as Merlin nimbly danced out of its way.

The snake shimmered and grew, returning to the shape of Lady Viviane. Only now she was a worn-out old hag with pure white hair and a bent and wrinkled body.

"What happened to her?" Dean asked

"She's so ugly!" Donna cried.

Lady Viviane turned haltingly toward Merlin. "I have but to utter one more phrase, Merlin," she said, her voice cracking, "and the curse of Nothtoad will be complete!"

"Viviane, don't," Merlin said. "No revenge is worth harming the innocent."

Lady Viviane shook her head defiantly. "You are wrong, old man!" She mumbled some strange words and the light around her changed from yellow to angry red. Beams of light shot out of her hands.

Merlin stepped toward her.

"You're too late, Merlin," Lady Viviane said with a cackle, "too late! I've won!"

The light flowed from her in a great roaring stream, brushing the ceiling.

Donna and Kari covered their ears.

The flags hanging from the rafters whipped around and the tapestry on the wall buckled and flapped. The light rolled down the walls.

Still roaring, the light flowed over the stones of the floor, bathing the room in a warm glow. The roar subsided, turning into the gentle sound of a brook. The light seemed to seep into the cracks between the stones.

A wide smile appeared on Merlin's face.

"Oh, no!" Lady Viviane shrieked. "Oh, no! I've been tri-i-i-ck-ed . . ."

Suddenly, the bright light went out and Lady Viviane dropped to the floor. The last eddy of light sank between the stones. The Great Hall was silent.

The teens looked at each other and then at Merlin. For a long moment he didn't move. Then he seemed to relax, all of the tension leaving his body.

"W-what happened?" Kari managed to stammer.

Percival strode over and kneeled down next to

Viviane. "She's sleeping, Sire," he announced.

"She should be out for decades," Merlin remarked, with a slight smile.

"But what about the Curse of Nothtoad?" Jeremy asked.

"It was my little joke," Merlin said. "I knew Viviane couldn't be trusted, so I made her believe that Nothtoad was the most powerful curse I could teach her. It is in a way, because it takes away all your power and gives it back to the earth, from whence it comes."

"So she outsmarted herself?" Dean asked.

"Yes," Merlin said, pulling on his beard. "Yes, that is a good way to put it. That's the problem with tricks. They sometimes end up tricking you."

"What will happen to her?" Elaine asked.

"She will sleep now and forget what happened," Merlin replied.

"And when she awakes she'll be back to her old tricks," Percival added.

"Perhaps," Merlin said thoughtfully, "but that won't be for a long, long time."

Percival lifted Viviane and carried her toward the stairway.

Merlin turned to the teens. "Thank you for your help," he said. "I could not have won without it . . . and your devices. They are really quite marvelous."

Merlin took the digital watch off his wrist. "Everything depended on just the right timing," he said as he handed the watch back to Trent.

"And this helped me fool Lady Viviane," he said, retrieving the radio from the corner. He handed it to Dean.

Then he held up the hair dryer. "This was the best of all, but I'm afraid I may have worn it out."

The hair dryer was a melted glob of plastic .

"It's all right," Donna said, "you can keep it."

"You were very brave," Merlin continued. "I think that the land is safe in your hands. Excalibur and I can rest a little longer." He turned away.

Jeremy reached toward Merlin. "But you have so much to tell us."

"Yeah," Kari added. "You could teach us how to do all that magic."

Merlin paused. "Magic is what you make of the world," he said. "Just try to make it better."

Merlin walked to the stairs and turned back. "You must sleep now," he said. "Try not to worry about what you have seen."

CHAPTER
24

A clanking sound caused the teens to stir. Bright daylight filled the minivan.

"Close the blinds," Donna said.

The clanking noise came again, followed by regular pings from a bell.

"What is that?" Trent said irritably, rubbing his eyes. He sat up and looked around.

"Shhh," Elaine said, "I feel like I could sleep for a thousand years."

Mr. Axelrod knocked on the window of the van. "Time to get up. We've got to get some breakfast."

Slowly the teens stretched and looked around. The van was parked in a roadside petrol station, across the road from a huge tree. The attendant stood at the rear of the minivan, putting gas into the tank. The morning sun was bright and the sky was cloudless.

Mr. Axelrod had a road map spread out on the hood of the minivan. "Maybe you can give me some directions," he said to the attendant. "But first check the engine, please. The battery seemed a little run down when I tried to start it this morning. I must've left the lights on."

The attendant was a large man with bright red hair and blue eyes, dressed in greasy overalls and heavy boots. He returned the nozzle to the gas pump and went to the front of the van. "Beggin' your pardon, guv'," he said, wiping his hands on an old rag. "I need to open the bonnet."

Mr. Axelrod pulled the map out of the way.

Dean and Kari climbed out of the van and stretched, trying to wake up. Jeremy and Trent joined them.

"Where are we, Mr. Axelrod?" Dean asked.

Mr. Axelrod straightened out the road map and pointed. "I think we're about here."

Dean and Jeremy looked where Mr. Axelrod was pointing on the map. "Boy, we were really lost last night," Dean said. "I thought we were somewhere over here." He pointed to another spot on the map.

"These roads are pretty tricky at night," Mr. Axelrod said.

"And in the rain," Jeremy added.

"This morning we'll drive about a hundred miles and see a real medieval castle," Mr. Axelrod announced, "one of the forts King Edward built to protect the English border from Welsh raiders. Then you can see some real history."

"Isn't there a castle near here?" Donna asked.

"Not according to the map," Mr. Axelrod replied. "We're miles from the nearest ruins."

Dean whispered to Jeremy, "Didn't we sleep in a castle last night?"

Trent overheard Dean. "What are you, nuts? We slept all night in the van."

The attendant leaned around the side of the van. "There are some ruins up on that hill," he said, pointing toward a small rise a short distance from the road, "but whatever walls there were tumbled down long ago. We had some archaeologist blokes down here a few years ago. They dug around a bit but didn't find anything. I've lived around here all my life. No castles near here." He ducked back under the hood.

Mr. Axelrod stepped to the front of the van with the map. "I just want to make sure we know where we are," he said to the attendant. "Can you show me on this map."

The attendant straightened up and looked at the

map. "I can't say that this place is on any map," he said, "on account of it being so small and all."

"Well, just show me about where it is," Mr. Axelrod insisted.

The attendant squinted at the map. "I'd say you were just about here," he said.

Mr. Axelrod peered closely at the map. "Is this place too new to be on a map?" he asked.

"Oh, no. It's a very old place," the attendant replied, "but a little out of the way. It goes by the name of Nothtoad."

Kari spun toward the attendant, "Nothtoad?"

"Yes," the attendant replied. "Have you heard of it? It is the best farmland in England. Crops grow like magic here."

Kari slowly shook her head. "No," she said, "I guess not . . . but it's such a strange name."

Elaine stepped out of the van. She looked very tired, with deep circles under her eyes.

"What happened to you?" Donna asked. "You look like you didn't sleep a wink."

Elaine shook her head. "I don't think I did. I kept having these weird dreams."

"Well, I slept like a log," Mr. Axelrod said, folding up the map. "Now before we go to that castle, I've got a real lesson in ecology for you. The air here used to be black with soot from furnaces and car

116

engines burning coal. One kind of moth adapted to the smoke by turning from white to black so its enemies couldn't see it on soot-covered trees. Then the British cleaned up the air and the moths responded over several generations by gradually turning white again. Isn't that an amazing story?"

"Didn't we hear something about moths last night?" Dean asked.

The others shrugged.

"I sort of remember," Trent said.

The attendant closed the hood. "That should do you, sir," he said to Mr. Axelrod. Mr. Axelrod paid him and they all got back in the van.

As the van started up, Jeremy looked out the window at the large tree. He shook his head. "I'm sure I remember something about last night."

Trent squirmed restlessly. "The only thing I remember is rain."

"No," Jeremy said. "Something else. I just can't remember . . . ."

"Has somebody got my hair dryer?" Donna asked from the back seat. She was pawing through her luggage. "I can't find it."

"Did you have it last night?" Kari asked. "Maybe you left it in London."

"I don't know," Donna replied softly. "I can't remember."

AFTERWORD

The legends of Merlin the Magician, King Arthur, and the Knights of the Round Table have been favorite stories for hundreds of years. A legend is a story handed down from earlier times that historians can't prove true or false, but legends often have some basis in historical fact. Although the details are lost in time, the legends of King Arthur may be based on events that took place during the Anglo-Saxon invasion of Britain in the sixth century, more than a thousand years ago.

Arthur is referred to as the King of the Britons in some stories. The Britons were a Celtic people living in Britain when the Anglo-Saxons invaded. Arthur may have been a leader during their long resistance against these invaders. Although the

Britons fought bravely, the Anglo-Saxons gradually pushed them west into Wales and Ireland and north into Scotland. In fact, a strong tradition of separateness from the English (a name which comes from the word Anglo) still survives in these regions today.

A number of places in England claim to be connected with Arthur, including Glastonbury, a real location near where our story takes place. Here in the late twelfth century, a group of monks claimed to have found the burial site of an ancient king and his queen. The monks believed that the king was Arthur and the queen Guinevere. There is also a chairlike shape in the rocks of a craggy volcano near Edinburgh, Scotland, that is known as Arthur's Seat. It is unlikely that Arthur ever sat there or that the monks were right about his tomb.

Merlin the Magician is a favorite character in the legends of Arthur. As a boy, he was called Emrys. Emrys foresaw the victory of Arthur's father, Uther Pendragon, over an evil king. When Uther was victorious, Emrys was made the chief advisor to King Uther and became known as Merlin. Merlin performed many services for Uther and was eventually rewarded by being made the guardian of Uther's son, Arthur. After Uther was killed in battle, Merlin hid the boy from harm and prepared him to be a wise and brave ruler.

To protect Arthur's throne while he was growing up, Merlin created the legendary sword in the stone. Whoever could pull the sword from an anvil on top of a stone would be the rightful king of the Britons. Because no one could budge the sword, there was no king. When Arthur became a young man, however, he was able to pull the sword free and eventually became king. Merlin was his chief advisor and helped King Arthur unite the Britons and gather together the Knights of the Round Table. He also built Arthur's castle, the beautiful Camelot, and at one time was thought to have magically created Stonehenge, the mysterious stone monument that still stands on Salisbury Plain.

Merlin supposedly had many powers, including the ability to change himself into various animals and to create music out of the air. He was also considered the guardian of the land of Britain, which in some legends is called "Merlin's Enclosure."

But Merlin also had his weaknesses. He was absentminded and sometimes a little cranky. The legends say that he was tricked by a young woman named Viviane, also known as Elaine, and trapped in an ice cave somewhere in the western part of England. There he sleeps, waiting to be awakened and called upon to perform his magic once more.

Why have the stories of Camelot and the

Knights of the Round Table remained so popular over the years? Perhaps because they tell us about the victory of good over evil. They remind us of the significance of the ideals of bravery and honesty and courtesy, and the importance of justice and fairness for all. If these ideals could be realized in the past, then we should strive to make them real today.

The legends of King Arthur also remind us that in times of great need, great leaders do step forward. Leaders such as Joan of Arc, Abraham Lincoln, or Martin Luther King take on the challenges of their time, sometimes at heroic cost. That may be why the legends of the great guardians, Arthur and Merlin, tell us that they are just sleeping, ready to return in times of great stress to set things right.

There are many excellent retellings of the stories of Arthur and Merlin. You may want to look at T. H. White's *The Once and Future King* and *The Book of Merlin*. For a funny look at a modern response to King Arthur, check out Mark Twain's *A Connecticut Yankee in King Arthur's Court*. Older sources of the Arthur legend include the writings of Sir Thomas Malory, Chretien De Troyes, and Geoffrey of Monmouth. All of these should be available at your local bookstore or library.

While the stories about Merlin may be imaginary, it is a fact that certain moths changed from white to black in Great Britain during the last one hundred years. This was a response to the increase in the amount of soot in the air produced by factories burning coal. White moths were more easily seen by predators on trees coated with coal dust than their black relatives. However, since the 1950's, increased environmental awareness has forced the factories to reduce pollutants. As the air has become much cleaner, these moths have gradually shifted back to their original white color. The mechanism that produced this change is called "industrial melanism" by scientists. It is one of the pieces of evidence pointing toward the dangers of air pollution.

The places seen by the teens in London are all real and you can visit them, too. The British Museum and the Tower of London should be high on any list of things to see. Although you are allowed to tour many castles in Great Britain, Merlin's Castle is entirely imaginary. So is the magic performed by Merlin and Lady Viviane. But remember, as Merlin said, "Magic is what you make of the world. Just try to make it better."

P. J. Stray

DANGER ON LIGHTHOUSE REEF

Twins Mike and Maddie Richards are not looking forward to attending their father's wedding in far-away Belize, but what could be more fun than a vacation in a tropical paradise? The days are sunny, the water is warm, and the snorkeling is excellent. But danger lurks in the coral reefs! Something is poisoning the coral and threatening the sea animals. Along with their new friend Brandon, who knows the reefs, they rescue a baby manatee that is sick with a mysterious illness. But that's just the beginning of the puzzle. Swimming makes Brandon sick, too, and frightening bright lights and terrifying noises in the night lead to more questions and clues to a sunken treasure.

There are perils in the deep and mysteries to be solved in *DANGER ON LIGHTHOUSE REEF*, the next Passport Mystery by P.J. Stray.

PASSPORT MYSTERIES TAKE YOU AROUND THE WORLD!

Look for your passport in A Passport Mystery #1 *Secrets in the Mayan Ruins* (paperback version only)

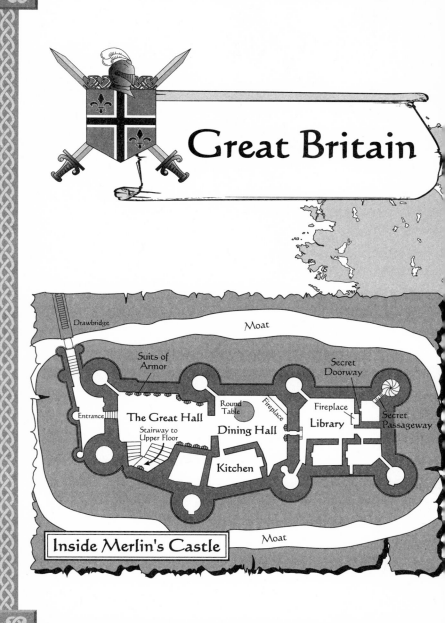

Great Britain

Drawbridge

Moat

Suits of Armor

Secret Doorway

Entrance

The Great Hall

Round Table

Fireplace

Fireplace

Library

Secret Passageway

Stairway to Upper Floor

Dining Hall

Kitchen

Moat

Inside Merlin's Castle